The Oxford Treasury of
CLASSIC POEMS

Past, Present, Future

Tell me, tell me, smiling child,
What the past is like to thee?
'An Autumn evening soft and mild
With a wind that sighs mournfully.'

Tell me, what is the present hour?
'A green and flowery spray
Where a young bird sits gathering its power
To mount and fly away.'

And what is the future, happy one?
'A sea beneath a cloudless sun;
A mighty, glorious, dazzling sea
Stretching into infinity.'

Emily Brontë

The Oxford Treasury of
CLASSIC
POEMS

Michael Harrison
and Christopher Stuart-Clark

Oxford University Press

Oxford New York Toronto

Prayer to Laughter

O Laughter
giver of relaxed mouths

you who rule our belly with tickles
you who come when not called
you who can embarrass us at times

send us stitches in our sides
shake us till the water reaches our eyes
buckle our knees till we cannot stand

we whose faces are grim and shattered
we whose hearts are no longer hearty
O Laughter we beg you

crack us up
crack us up

John Agard

Contents

Tartary

If I were Lord of Tartary,
　Myself and me alone,
My bed should be of ivory,
　Of beaten gold my throne;
And in my court should peacocks flaunt,
And in my forests tigers haunt,
And in my pools great fishes slant
　Their fins athwart the sun.

If I were Lord of Tartary,
　Trumpeters every day
To every meal would summon me,
　And in my courtyard bray;
And in the evening lamps would shine,
Yellow as honey, red as wine,
While harp, and flute, and mandoline,
　Made music sweet and gay.

If I were Lord of Tartary,
　I'd wear a robe of beads,
White, and gold, and green they'd be—
　And clustered thick as seeds;
And ere should wane the morning-star,
I'd don my robe and scimitar,
And zebras seven should draw my car
　Through Tartary's dark glades.

Lord of the fruits of Tartary,
　Her rivers silver-pale!
Lord of the hills of Tartary,
　Glen, thicket, wood, and dale!
Her flashing stars, her scented breeze,
Her trembling lakes, like foamless seas,
Her bird-delighting citron-trees
　In every purple vale!

Walter de la Mare

The Owl and the Pussy-Cat

The Owl and the Pussy-Cat went to sea
   In a beautiful pea-green boat,
They took some honey, and plenty of money,
   Wrapped up in a five-pound note.
The Owl looked up to the stars above,
   And sang to a small guitar,
'O lovely Pussy! O Pussy, my love,
   What a beautiful Pussy you are,
      You are,
      You are!
   What a beautiful Pussy you are!'

Pussy said to the Owl, 'You elegant fowl!
   How charmingly sweet you sing!
O let us be married! too long we have tarried:
   But what shall we do for a ring?'
They sailed away for a year and a day,
   To the land where the Bong-tree grows,
And there in a wood a Piggy-wig stood,
   With a ring at the end of his nose,
      His nose,
      His nose,
   With a ring at the end of his nose.

'Dear Pig, are you willing to sell for one shilling
     Your ring?' Said the Piggy, 'I will.'
So they took it away, and were married next day
     By the Turkey who lives on the hill.
They dined on mince, and slices of quince,
     Which they ate with a runcible spoon;
And hand in hand, on the edge of the sand,
     They danced by the light of the moon,
               The moon,
               The moon,
     They danced by the light of the moon.

Edward Lear

The Cat and the Moon

The cat went here and there
And the moon spun round like a top,
And the nearest kin of the moon,
The creeping cat, looked up.
Black Minnaloushe stared at the moon,
For, wander and wail as he would,
The pure cold light in the sky
Troubled his animal blood.
Minnaloushe runs in the grass
Lifting his delicate feet.
Do you dance, Minnaloushe, do you dance?
When two close kindred meet,
What better than call a dance?
Maybe the moon may learn,
Tired of that courtly fashion,
A new dance turn.
Minnaloushe creeps through the grass
From moonlit place to place,
The sacred moon overhead
Has taken a new phase.
Does Minnaloushe know that his pupils
Will pass from change to change,
And that from round to crescent,
From crescent to round they range?
Minnaloushe creeps through the grass
Alone, important and wise,
And lifts to the changing moon
His changing eyes.

W. B. Yeats

January Jumps About

January jumps about
in the frying pan
trying to heat
his frozen feet
like a Canadian.

February scuttles under
any dish's lid
and she thinks she's dry because she's
thoroughly well hid
but it still rains all month long
and it always did.

March sits in the bath tub
with the taps turned on.
Hot and cold, cold or not,
Has the winter gone?
In like a lion, out like a lamb
March on, march on, march on.

April slips about
sometimes indoors
and sometimes out
sometimes sheltering from a little
shower of bright rain
in an empty milk bottle
then dashing out again.

May, she hides nowhere,
nowhere at all.
Proud as a peacock
walking by a wall.
The Maytime O the Maytime
full of leaf and flower
The Maytime O the Maytime
is loveliest of all.

June discards his shirt and
trousers by the stream
and takes the first dip of the year
into a jug of cream.
June is the gay time
of every girl and boy
who run about and sing and shout
in pardonable joy.

July by the sea
sits dabbling with sand
letting it run out of
her rather lazy hand,
and sometimes she sadly
thinks: 'As I sit here
ah, more than half the year is gone,
the evanescent year.'

August by an emperor
was given his great name.
It is gold and purple
like a Hall of Fame.
(I have known it rather cold
and wettish, all the same.)

September lies in shadows
of the fading summer
hearing, in the distance,
the silver horns of winter
and not very far off
the coming autumn drummer.

October, October
apples on the tree,
the partridge in the wood and
the big winds at sea,
the mud beginning in the lane
the berries bright and red
and the big tree wildly
tossing its old head.

November when the fires
love to burn, and leaves
flit about and fill the air
where the old tree grieves.
November, November
its name is like a star
glittering on many things that were
but few things that are.

Twelfth and last December.
A few weeks away
we hear the silver bells
of the stag and the sleigh
flying from the tundras
far far away
bringing to us all the gift
of our Christmas Day.

George Barker

15

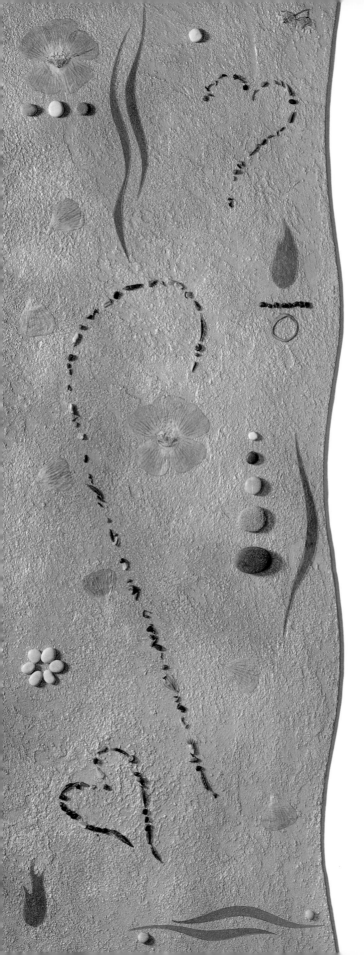

Spell of Creation

Within the flower there lies a seed,
Within the seed there springs a tree,
Within the tree there spreads a wood.

In the wood there burns a fire,
And in the fire there melts a stone,
Within the stone a ring of iron.

Within the ring there lies an O
Within the O there looks an eye,
In the eye there swims a sea,

And in the sea reflected sky,
And in the sky there shines the sun,
Within the sun a bird of gold.

Within the bird there beats a heart,
And from the heart there flows a song,
And in the song there sings a word.

In the word there speaks a world,
A word of joy, a world of grief,
From joy and grief there springs my love.

Oh love, my love, there springs a world,
And on the world there shines a sun
And in the sun there burns a fire,

Within the fire consumes my heart
And in my heart there beats a bird,
And in the bird there wakes an eye,

Within the eye, earth, sea and sky,
Earth, sky and sea within an O
Lie like the seed within the flower.

Kathleen Raine

Pied Beauty

Glory be to God for dappled things—
    For skies of couple-colour as a brindled cow;
      For rose-moles all in stipple upon trout that swim;
Fresh-firecoal chestnut-falls; finches' wings;
    Landscape plotted and pieced—fold, fallow, and plough;
      And all trades, their gear and tackle and trim.
All things counter, original, spare, strange;
    Whatever is fickle, freckled (who knows how?)
      With swift, slow; sweet, sour; adazzle, dim;
He fathers-forth whose beauty is past change:
           Praise him.

Gerard Manley Hopkins

from 'Lines Composed a Few Miles above Tintern Abbey'

                    The sounding cataract
Haunted me like a passion: the tall rock,
The mountain, and the deep and gloomy wood,
Their colours and their forms, were then to me
An appetite; a feeling and a love,
That had no need of a remoter charm,
By thought supplied, nor any interest
Unborrowed from the eye.—That time is past,
And all its aching joys are now no more,
And all its dizzy raptures. Not for this
Faint I, nor mourn nor murmur; other gifts
Have followed; for such loss, I would believe,
Abundant recompense. For I have learned
To look on nature, not as in the hour
Of thoughtless youth; but hearing oftentimes
The still, sad music of humanity,
Nor harsh nor grating, though of ample power
To chasten and subdue. And I have felt
A presence that disturbs me with the joy
Of elevated thoughts; a sense sublime
Of something far more deeply interfused,
Whose dwelling is the light of setting suns,
And the round ocean and the living air,
And the blue sky, and in the mind of man:

A motion and a spirit, that impels
All thinking things, all objects of all thought,
And rolls through all things. Therefore am I still
A lover of the meadows and the woods,
And mountains; and of all that we behold
From this green earth; of all the mighty world
Of eye, and ear,—both what they half create,
And what perceive; well pleased to recognize
In nature and the language of the sense
The anchor of my purest thoughts, the nurse,
The guide, the guardian of my heart, and soul
Of all my moral being.

William Wordsworth

The Wild Swans at Coole

The trees are in their autumn beauty,
The woodland paths are dry,
Under the October twilight the water
Mirrors a still sky;
Upon the brimming water among the stones
Are nine-and-fifty swans.

The nineteenth autumn has come upon me
Since I first made my count;
I saw, before I had well finished,
All suddenly mount
And scatter wheeling in great broken rings
Upon their clamorous wings.

I have looked upon those brilliant creatures,
And now my heart is sore.
All's changed since I, hearing at twilight,
The first time on this shore,
The bell-beat of their wings above my head,
Trod with a lighter tread.

Unwearied still, lover by lover,
They paddle in the cold
Companionable streams or climb the air;
Their hearts have not grown old;
Passion and conquest, wander where they will,
Attend upon them still.

But now they drift on the still water,
Mysterious, beautiful;
Among what rushes will they build,
By what lake's edge or pool
Delight men's eyes when I awake some day
To find they have flown away?

W. B. Yeats

21

The Galloping Cat

Oh I am a cat that likes to
Gallop about doing good
So
One day when I was
Galloping about doing good, I saw
A Figure in the path; I said:
Get off! (Be-
  cause
I am a cat that likes to
Gallop about doing good)
But he did not move, instead
He raised his hand as if
To land me a cuff
So I made to dodge so as to
Prevent him bringing it orf,
Un-for-tune-ately I slid
On a banana skin
Some Ass had left instead
Of putting in the bin. So
His hand caught me on the cheek
I tried
To lay his arm open from wrist to elbow
With my sharp teeth
Because I am
A cat that likes to gallop about doing good.
Would you believe it?
He wasn't there
My teeth met nothing but air,
But a Voice said: Poor cat,
(Meaning me) and a soft stroke
Came on me head
Since when I have been bald.
I regard myself as
A martyr to doing good.

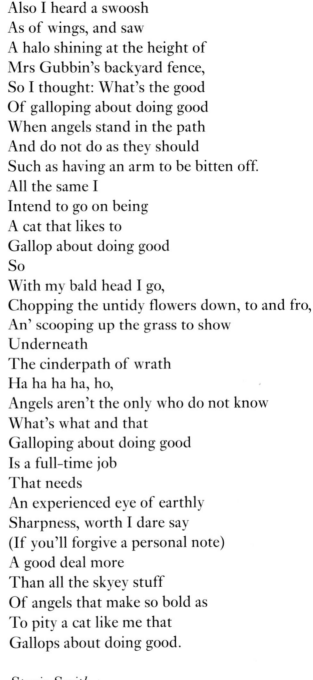

Also I heard a swoosh
As of wings, and saw
A halo shining at the height of
Mrs Gubbin's backyard fence,
So I thought: What's the good
Of galloping about doing good
When angels stand in the path
And do not do as they should
Such as having an arm to be bitten off.
All the same I
Intend to go on being
A cat that likes to
Gallop about doing good
So
With my bald head I go,
Chopping the untidy flowers down, to and fro,
An' scooping up the grass to show
Underneath
The cinderpath of wrath
Ha ha ha ha, ho,
Angels aren't the only who do not know
What's what and that
Galloping about doing good
Is a full-time job
That needs
An experienced eye of earthly
Sharpness, worth I dare say
(If you'll forgive a personal note)
A good deal more
Than all the skyey stuff
Of angels that make so bold as
To pity a cat like me that
Gallops about doing good.

Stevie Smith

from 'Auguries of Innocence'

A Robin Redbreast in a cage
Puts all Heaven in a rage.

A Dove house filled with Doves and Pigeons
Shudders hell through all its regions.

A Dog starved at his master's gate
Predicts the ruin of the state.

A Horse misused upon the road
Calls to Heaven for human blood.

Each outcry of the hunted Hare
A fibre from the brain does tear.

A Skylark wounded in the wing,
A cherubin does cease to sing.

The Game Cock clipped and armed for fight
Does the rising sun affright.

Every Wolf's and Lion's howl
Raises from hell a human soul.

The wild Deer wand'ring here and there
Keeps the human soul from care.

The Lamb misused breeds public strife
And yet forgives the butcher's knife.

The Bat that flits at close of eve
Has left the brain that won't believe.

The Owl that calls upon the night
Speaks the unbeliever's fright.

William Blake

The Eagle

He clasps the crag with crooked hands;
Close to the sun in lonely lands,
Ring'd with the azure world, he stands.

The wrinkled sea beneath him crawls;
He watches from his mountain walls,
And like a thunderbolt he falls.

Alfred, Lord Tennyson

The Donkey

When fishes flew and forests walked
    And figs grew upon thorn,
Some moment when the moon was blood
    Then surely I was born;

With monstrous head and sickening cry
    And ears like errant wings,
The devil's walking parody
    On all four-footed things.

The tattered outlaw of the earth,
    Of ancient crooked will;
Starve, scourge, deride me: I am dumb,
    I keep my secret still.

Fools! For I also had my hour;
    One far fierce hour and sweet:
There was a shout about my ears,
    And palms before my feet.

G. K. Chesterton

Inversnaid

This darksome burn, horseback brown,
His rollrock highroad roaring down,
In coop and in comb the fleece of his foam
Flutes and low to the lake falls home.

A windpuff-bonnet of fawn-froth
Turns and twindles over the broth
Of a pool so pitchblack, fell-frowning,
It rounds and rounds Despair to drowning.

Degged with dew, dappled with dew
Are the groins of the braes that the brook treads through,
Wiry heathpacks, flitches of fern,
And the beadbonny ash that sits over the burn.

What would the world be, once bereft
Of wet and of wildness? Let them be left,
O let them be left, wildness and wet;
Long live the weeds and the wilderness yet.

Gerard Manley Hopkins

Horses on the Camargue

In the grey wastes of dread,
The haunt of shattered gulls where nothing moves
But in a shroud of silence like the dead,
I heard a sudden harmony of hooves,
And, turning, saw afar
A hundred snowy horses unconfined,
The silver runaways of Neptune's car
Racing, spray curled, like waves before the wind.
Sons of the Mistral, fleet
As him with whose strong gusts they love to flee,
Who shod the flying thunders on their feet
And plumed them with the snortings of the sea;
Theirs is no earthly breed
Who only haunt the verges of the earth
And only on the sea's salt herbage feed—
Surely the great white breakers gave them birth.
For when for years a slave,
A horse of the Camargue, in alien lands,
Should catch some far-off fragrance of the wave
Carried far inland from his native sands,
Many have told the tale
Of how in fury, foaming at the rein,
He hurls his rider; and with lifted tail,
With coal-red eyes and cataracting mane,

Heading his course for home,
Though sixty foreign leagues before him sweep,
Will never rest until he breathes the foam
And hears the native thunder of the deep.
But when the great gusts rise
And lash their anger on these arid coasts,
When the scared gulls career with mournful cries
And whirl across the waste like driven ghosts:
When hail and fire converge,
The only souls to which they strike no pain
Are the white-crested fillies of the surge
And the white horses of the windy plain.
Then in their strength and pride
The stallions of the wilderness rejoice;
They feel their Master's trident in their side,
And high and shrill they answer to his voice.
With white tails smoking free,
Long streaming manes, and arching necks, they show
Their kinship to their sisters of the sea—
And forward hurl their thunderbolts of snow.
Still out of hardship bred,
Spirits of power and beauty and delight
Have ever on such frugal pastures fed
And loved to course with tempests through the night.

Roy Campbell

My Heart's in the Highlands

My heart's in the Highlands, my heart is not here;
My heart's in the Highlands a-chasing the deer;
Chasing the wild deer, and following the roe,
My heart's in the Highlands wherever I go.
Farewell to the Highlands, farewell to the North,
The birth-place of valour, the country of worth;
Wherever I wander, wherever I rove,
The hills of the Highlands for ever I love.

Farewell to the mountains, high covered with snow;
Farewell to the straths and green valleys below;
Farewell to the forests and wild-hanging woods;
Farewell to the torrents and loud-pouring floods.
My heart's in the Highlands, my heart is not here;
My heart's in the Highlands a-chasing the deer;
Chasing the wild deer, and following the roe,
My heart's in the Highlands, wherever I go.

Robert Burns

Home Thoughts, from Abroad

Oh, to be in England
Now that April's there,
And whoever wakes in England
Sees, some morning, unaware,
That the lowest boughs and the brushwood sheaf
Round the elm-tree bole are in tiny leaf,
While the chaffinch sings on the orchard bough,
In England—now.

And after April, when May follows,
And the whitethroat builds, and all the swallows,
Hark! where my blossomed pear-tree in the hedge
Leans to the field and scatters on the clover
Blossoms and dewdrops—at the bent spray's edge—
That's the wise thrush; he sings each song twice over,
Lest you should think he never could recapture
The first fine careless rapture!
And though the fields look rough with hoary dew,
All will be gay when noontide wakes anew
The buttercups, the little children's dower,
—Far brighter than this gaudy melon-flower!

Robert Browning

A Martian Sends a Postcard Home

Caxtons are mechanical birds with many wings
and some are treasured for their markings—

they cause the eyes to melt
or the body to shriek without pain.

I have never seen one fly, but
sometimes they perch on the hand.

Mist is when the sky is tired of flight
and rests its soft machine on ground:

then the world is dim and bookish
like engravings under tissue paper.

Rain is when the earth is television.
It has the property of making colours darker.

Model T is a room with the lock inside—
a key is turned to free the world

for movement, so quick there is a film
to watch for anything missed.

But time is tied to the wrist
or kept in a box, ticking with impatience.

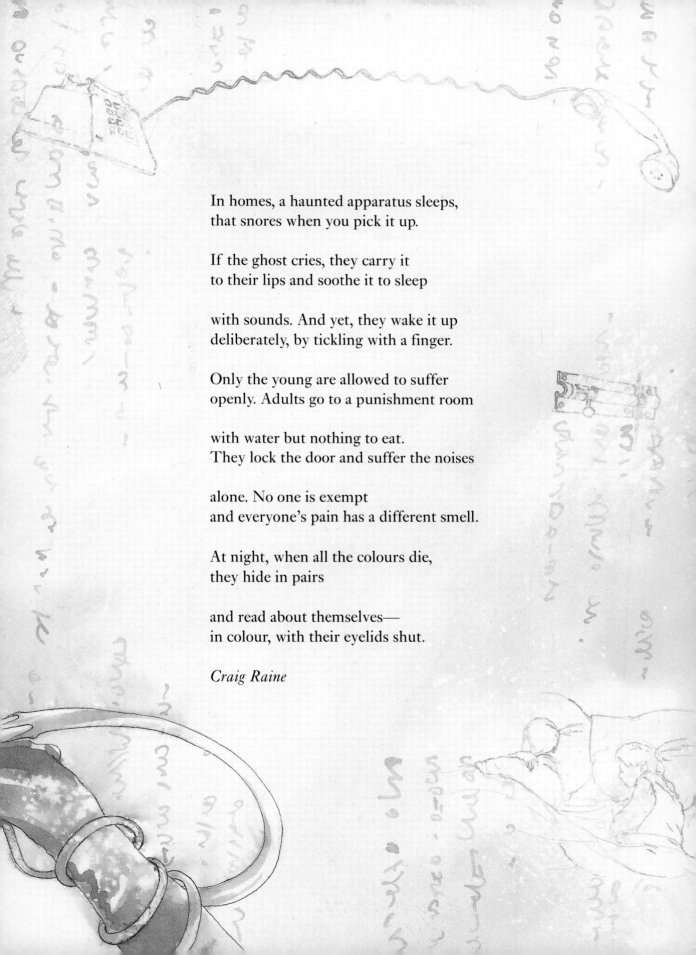

In homes, a haunted apparatus sleeps,
that snores when you pick it up.

If the ghost cries, they carry it
to their lips and soothe it to sleep

with sounds. And yet, they wake it up
deliberately, by tickling with a finger.

Only the young are allowed to suffer
openly. Adults go to a punishment room

with water but nothing to eat.
They lock the door and suffer the noises

alone. No one is exempt
and everyone's pain has a different smell.

At night, when all the colours die,
they hide in pairs

and read about themselves—
in colour, with their eyelids shut.

Craig Raine

No!

No sun — no moon!
No morn — no noon —
No dawn — no dusk — no proper time of day —
No sky — no earthly view —
No distance looking blue —
No road — no street — no 't'other side the way' —
No end to any Row —
No indications where the Crescents go —
No top to any steeple —
No recognitions of familiar people —
No courtesies for showing 'em —
No knowing 'em! —
No travelling at all — no locomotion,
No inkling of the way — no notion —
'No go' — by land or ocean —
No mail — no post —
No news from any foreign coast —
No Park — no Ring — no afternoon gentility —
No company — no nobility —
No warmth, no cheerfulness, no healthful ease,
No comfortable feel in any member —
No shade, no shine, no butterflies, no bees,
No fruits, no flowers, no leaves, no birds, —
November!

Thomas Hood

BC:AD

This was the moment when Before
Turned into After, and the future's
Uninvented timekeepers presented arms.

This was the moment when nothing
Happened. Only dull peace
Sprawled boringly over the earth.

This was the moment when even energetic Romans
Could find nothing better to do
Than counting heads in remote provinces.

And this was the moment
When a few farm workers and three
Members of an obscure Persian sect

Walked haphazard by starlight straight
Into the kingdom of heaven.

U. A. Fanthorpe

Kubla Khan

In Xanadu did Kubla Khan
   A stately pleasure-dome decree:
Where Alph, the sacred river, ran
Through caverns measureless to man
   Down to a sunless sea.
So twice five miles of fertile ground
With walls and towers were girdled round:
And here were gardens bright with sinuous rills,
Where blossomed many an incense-bearing tree;
And here were forests ancient as the hills,
Enfolding sunny spots of greenery.

But Oh! that deep romantic chasm which slanted
Down the green hill athwart a cedarn cover!
A savage place! as holy and enchanted
As e'er beneath a waning moon was haunted
By woman wailing for her demon-lover!
And from this chasm, with ceaseless turmoil seething,
As if this Earth in fast thick pants were breathing,
A mighty fountain momently was forced:
Amid whose swift half-intermitted burst
Huge fragments vaulted like rebounding hail,
Or chaffy grain beneath the thresher's flail:
And 'mid these dancing rocks at once and ever
It flung up momently the sacred river.

Five miles meandering with a mazy motion
Through wood and dale the sacred river ran,
Then reached the caverns measureless to man,
And sank in tumult to a lifeless ocean:
And 'mid this tumult Kubla heard from far
Ancestral voices prophesying war!
    The shadow of the dome of pleasure
    Floated midway on the waves;
    Where was heard the mingled measure
    From the fountain and the caves.
It was a miracle of rare device,
A sunny pleasure-dome with caves of ice!

    A damsel with a dulcimer
    In a vision once I saw:
    It was an Abyssinian maid,
    And on her dulcimer she played,
    Singing of Mount Abora.
Could I revive within me
Her symphony and song,
To such a deep delight 'twould win me
That with music loud and long,
I would build that dome in air,
That sunny dome! those caves of ice!
And all who heard should see them there,
And all should cry, Beware! Beware!
His flashing eyes, his floating hair!
Weave a circle round him thrice,
And close your eyes with holy dread,
For he on honey-dew hath fed,
And drunk the milk of Paradise.

Samuel Taylor Coleridge

London

I wander thro' each charter'd street,
Near where the charter'd Thames does flow,
And mark in every face I meet
Marks of weakness, marks of woe.

In every cry of every Man,
In every Infant's cry of fear,
In every voice, in every ban,
The mind-forg'd manacles I hear.

How the Chimney-sweeper's cry
Every black'ning Church appalls;
And the hapless soldier's sigh
Runs in blood down Palace walls.

But most thro' midnight streets I hear
How the youthful Harlot's curse
Blasts the new born Infant's tear,
And blights with plagues the Marriage hearse.

William Blake

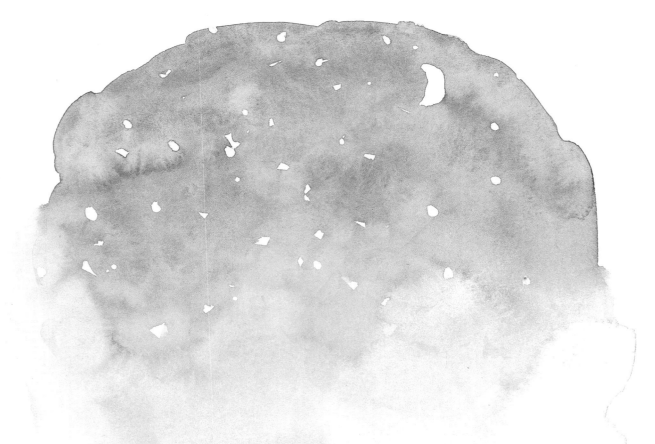

The Embankment

(The Fantasia of a Fallen Gentleman on a Cold, Bitter Night)

Once, in finesse of fiddles found I ecstasy,
In a flash of gold heels on the hard pavement.
Now see I
That warmth's the very stuff of poesy.
Oh, God, make small
The old star-eaten blanket of the sky,
That I may fold it round me and in comfort lie.

T. E. Hulme

Summer Recorded

We have a tape recorder that plays slower than it should,
gives back the notes of a piano lingering honeyed on the air,
guitars as musky fruit from an enchanted wood,
and flutes as tremulous sad maidens bright with golden hair;
each sounded moment lasts a fraction longer than the beat
of seconds spun out by the clock's unwavering steel.

I have known days like that, of warm winds drowsing in the heat
of noon and all of summer spinning slowly on its reel,
days briefly lived, that leave long music in the mind
more sweet than truth; I play them and rewind.

Russell Hoban

Snake

A snake came to my water-trough
On a hot, hot day, and I in pyjamas for the heat,
To drink there.

In the deep, strange-scented shade of the great dark carob-tree
I came down the steps with my pitcher
And must wait, must stand and wait, for there he was at the trough before me.

He reached down from a fissure in the earth-wall in the gloom
And trailed his yellow-brown slackness soft-bellied down, over the edge of the stone trough
And rested his throat upon the stone bottom,
And where the water had dripped from the tap, in a small clearness,
He sipped with his straight mouth,
Softly drank through his straight gums, into his slack long body,
Silently.
Someone was before me at my water-trough,
And I, like a second comer, waiting.

He lifted his head from his drinking, as cattle do,
And looked at me vaguely, as drinking cattle do,
And flickered his two-forked tongue from his lips, and mused a moment,
And stooped and drank a little more,
Being earth-brown, earth-golden from the burning bowels of the earth
On the day of Sicilian July, with Etna smoking.

The voice of my education said to me
He must be killed,
For in Sicily the black, black snakes are innocent, the gold are venomous.
And voices in me said, If you were a man
You would take a stick and break him now, and finish him off.

But must I confess how I liked him,
How glad I was he had come like a guest in quiet, to drink at my water-trough
And depart peaceful, pacified, and thankless,
Into the burning bowels of this earth?

Was it cowardice, that I dared not kill him?
Was it perversity, that I longed to talk to him?
Was it humility, to feel so honoured?
I felt so honoured.

And yet those voices:
If you were not afraid, you would kill him!

And truly I was afraid, I was most afraid,
But even so, honoured still more
That he should seek my hospitality
From out the dark door of the secret earth.

He drank enough
And lifted his head, dreamily, as one who has drunken,
And flickered his tongue like a forked night on the air, so black;
Seeming to lick his lips,
And looked around like a god, unseeing, into the air,
And slowly turned his head,
And slowly, very slowly, as if thrice adream,
Proceeded to draw his slow length curving round
And climb again the broken bank of my wall-face.

And as he put his head into that dreadful hole,
And as he slowly drew up, snake-easing his shoulders, and entered farther,
A sort of horror, a sort of protest against his withdrawing into that horrid black hole,
Deliberately going into the blackness, and slowly drawing himself after,
Overcame me now his back was turned.

I looked round, I put down my pitcher,
I picked up a clumsy log
And threw it at the water-trough with a clatter.

I think it did not hit him,
But suddenly that part of him that was left behind convulsed in undignified haste,
Writhed like lightning, and was gone
Into the black hole, the earth-lipped fissure in the wall-front,
At which, in the intense still noon, I stared with fascination.

And immediately I regretted it.
I thought how paltry, how vulgar, what a mean act!
I despised myself and the voices of my accursed human education.

And I thought of the albatross,
And I wished he would come back, my snake.

For he seemed to me again like a king,
Like a king in exile, uncrowned in the underworld,
Now due to be crowned again.

And so, I missed my chance with one of the lords
Of life.
And I have something to expiate;
A pettiness.

D. H. Lawrence

The Flower-fed Buffaloes

The flower-fed buffaloes of the spring
In the days of long ago,
Ranged where the locomotives sing
And the prairie flowers lie low:—
The tossing, blooming, perfumed grass
Is swept away by the wheat,
Wheels and wheels and wheels spin by
In the spring that still is sweet.
But the flower-fed buffaloes of the spring
Left us, long ago.
They gore no more, they bellow no more,
They trundle around the hills no more:—
With the Blackfeet, lying low,
With the Pawnees, lying low,
Lying low.

Vachel Lindsay

Adlestrop

Yes. I remember Adlestrop—
The name, because one afternoon
Of heat the express-train drew up there
Unwontedly. It was late June.

The steam hissed. Some one cleared his throat.
No one left and no one came
On the bare platform. What I saw
Was Adlestrop—only the name

And willows, willow-herb, and grass,
And meadowsweet, and haycocks dry,
No whit less still and lonely fair
Than the high cloudlets in the sky.

And for that minute a blackbird sang
Close by, and round him, mistier,
Farther and farther, all the birds
Of Oxfordshire and Gloucestershire.

Edward Thomas

Waving at Trains

Do people who wave at trains
Wave at the driver, or at the train itself?
Or, do people who wave at trains
Wave at the passengers? Those hurtling strangers,
The unidentifiable flying faces?

They must think we like being waved at.
Children do perhaps, and alone
In a compartment, the occasional passenger
Who is himself a secret waver at trains.
But most of us are unimpressed.

Some even think they're daft.
Stuck out there in a field, grinning.
But our ignoring them, our blank faces,
Even our pulled tongues and up you signs
Come three miles further down the line.

Out of harm's way by then
They continue their walk.
Refreshed and made pure, by the mistaken belief
That their love has been returned,
Because they have not seen it rejected.

It's like God in a way. Another day
Another universe. Always off somewhere.
And left behind, the faithful few,
Stuck out there. Not a care in the world.
All innocence. Arms in the air. Waving.

Roger McGough

The Night Mail

This is the night mail crossing the border,
Bringing the cheque and the postal order,
Letters for the rich, letters for the poor,
The shop at the corner and the girl next door,
Pulling up Beattock, a steady climb—
The gradient's against her but she's on time.

Past cotton grass and moorland boulder,
Shovelling white steam over her shoulder,
Snorting noisily as she passes
Silent miles of wind-bent grasses;
Birds turn their heads as she approaches,
Stare from the bushes at her blank-faced coaches;
Sheepdogs cannot turn her course,
They slumber on with paws across;
In the farm she passes no one wakes
But a jug in a bedroom gently shakes.

Dawn freshens, the climb is done.
Down towards Glasgow she descends
Towards the steam tugs, yelping down the glade of cranes
Towards the fields of apparatus, the furnaces
Set on the dark plain like gigantic chessmen.
All Scotland waits for her;
In the dark glens, beside the pale-green sea lochs,
Men long for news.

Letters of thanks, letters from banks,
Letters of joy from the girl and boy,
Receipted bills and invitations
To inspect new stock or visit relations,
And applications for situations,
And timid lovers' declarations,
And gossip, gossip from all the nations,
News circumstantial, news financial,
Letters with holiday snaps to enlarge in,
Letters with faces scrawled on the margin.
Letters from uncles, cousins and aunts,
Letters to Scotland from the South of France,
Letters of condolence to Highlands and Lowlands,
Notes from overseas to the Hebrides;
Written on paper of every hue,
The pink, the violet, the white and the blue,
The chatty, the catty, the boring, adoring,
The cold and official and the heart's outpouring,
Clever, stupid, short and long,
The typed and the printed and the spelt all wrong.

Thousands are still asleep
Dreaming of terrifying monsters
Or a friendly tea beside the band at Cranston's or Crawford's;
Asleep in working Glasgow, asleep in well-set Edinburgh,
Asleep in granite Aberdeen.
They continue their dreams
But shall wake soon and long for letters.
And none will hear the postman's knock
Without a quickening of the heart,
For who can bear to feel himself forgotten?

W. H. Auden

from 'The Rubaiyat of Omar Khayyam'

Awake! for Morning in the Bowl of Night
Has flung the Stone that puts the Stars to Flight:
   And lo! the Hunter of the East has caught
The Sultan's Turret in a Noose of Light.

Come, fill the Cup, and in the Fire of Spring
The Winter Garment of Repentance fling:
   The Bird of Time has but a little way
To fly—and Lo! the Bird is on the Wing.

        *   *   *

Here with a Loaf of Bread beneath the Bough,
A Flask of Wine, a Book of Verse—and Thou
   Beside me singing in the Wilderness—
And Wilderness is Paradise enow.

Think, in this battered Caravanserai
Whose Doorways are alternate Night and Day,
   How Sultan after Sultan with his Pomp
Abode his Hour or two, and went his way.

        *   *   *

Myself when young did eagerly frequent
Doctor and Saint, and heard great Argument
   About it and about, but evermore
Came out by the same Door as in I went.

Ah, fill the Cup:—what boots it to repeat
How time is slipping underneath our Feet:
   Unborn TO-MORROW and dead YESTERDAY,
Why fret about them if TO-DAY be sweet!

The Moving Finger writes; and, having writ,
Moves on; nor all your Piety nor Wit
   Shall lure it back to cancel half a line,
Nor all your Tears wash out a word of it.

Edward Fitzgerald

Sonnet LX

Like as the waves make towards the pebbled shore,
So do our minutes hasten to their end;
Each changing place with that which goes before,
In sequent toil all forwards do contend.
Nativity, once in the main of light,
Crawls to maturity, wherewith being crown'd,
Crooked eclipses 'gainst his glory fight,
And Time that gave doth now his gift confound.
Time doth transfix the flourish set on youth
And delves the parallels in beauty's brow,
Feeds on the rarities of nature's truth,
And nothing stands but for his scythe to mow:
  And yet to times in hope my verse shall stand,
  Praising thy worth, despite his cruel hand.

William Shakespeare

Death, Be Not Proud

Death, be not proud, though some have callèd thee
Mighty and dreadful, for thou art not so:
For those whom thou think'st thou dost overthrow
Die not, poor Death; nor yet canst thou kill me.
From Rest and Sleep, which but thy pictures be,
Much pleasure, then from thee much more must flow;
And soonest our best men with thee do go—
Rest of their bones and souls' delivery.
Thou'rt slave to fate, chance, kings, and desperate men,
And dost with poison, war, and sickness dwell;
And poppy or charms can make us sleep as well
And better than thy stroke. Why swell'st thou then?
One short sleep past, we wake eternally,
And Death shall be no more: Death, thou shalt die.

John Donne

To His Coy Mistress

Had we but world enough, and time,
This coyness, Lady, were no crime.
We would sit down and think which way
To walk and pass our long love's day.
Thou by the Indian Ganges' side
Shouldst rubies find: I by the tide
Of Humber would complain. I would
Love you ten years before the Flood,
And you should, if you please, refuse
Till the conversion of the Jews.
My vegetable love should grow
Vaster than empires, and more slow;
An hundred years should go to praise
Thine eyes and on thy forehead gaze;
Two hundred to adore each breast;
But thirty thousand to the rest;
An age at least to every part,
And the last age should show your heart;
For, Lady, you deserve this state,
Nor would I love at lower rate.

   But at my back I always hear
Time's wingèd chariot hurrying near;
And yonder all before us lie
Deserts of vast eternity.
Thy beauty shall no more be found,
Nor, in thy marble vault, shall sound
My echoing song: then worms shall try
That long preserv'd virginity,
And your quaint honour turn to dust,
And into ashes all my lust:
The grave's a fine and private place,
But none, I think, do there embrace.

Now therefore, while the youthful hue
Sits on thy skin like morning dew,
And while thy willing soul transpires
At every pore with instant fires,
Now let us sport us while we may,
And now, like amorous birds of prey,
Rather at once our time devour
Than languish in his slow-chapt power.
Let us roll all our strength and all
Our sweetness up into one ball,
And tear our pleasures with rough strife
Thorough the iron gates of life:
Thus, though we cannot make our sun
Stand still, yet we will make him run.

Andrew Marvell

Dover Beach

The sea is calm to-night.
The tide is full, the moon lies fair
Upon the straits;—on the French coast the light
Gleams and is gone; the cliffs of England stand,
Glimmering and vast, out in the tranquil bay.
Come to the window, sweet is the night-air!
Only, from the long line of spray
Where the sea meets the moon-blanch'd land,
Listen! you hear the grating roar
Of pebbles which the waves draw back, and fling,
At their return, up the high strand,
Begin, and cease, and then again begin,
With tremulous cadence slow, and bring
The eternal note of sadness in.

Sophocles long ago
Heard it on the Aegean, and it brought
Into his mind the turbid ebb and flow
Of human misery; we
Find also in the sound a thought,
Hearing it by this distant northern sea.

The Sea of Faith
Was once, too, at the full, and round earth's shore
Lay like the folds of a bright girdle furl'd.
But now I only hear
Its melancholy, long, withdrawing roar,
Retreating, to the breath
Of the night-wind, down the vast edges drear
And naked shingles of the world.

Ah, love, let us be true
To one another! for the world, which seems
To lie before us like a land of dreams,
So various, so beautiful, so new,
Hath really neither joy, nor love, nor light,
Nor certitude, nor peace, nor help for pain;
And we are here as on a darkling plain
Swept with confused alarms of struggle and flight,
Where ignorant armies clash by night.

Matthew Arnold

An Arundel Tomb

Side by side, their faces blurred,
The earl and countess lie in stone,
Their proper habits vaguely shown
As jointed armour, stiffened pleat,
And that faint hint of the absurd—
The little dogs under their feet.

Such plainness of the pre-baroque
Hardly involves the eye, until
It meets his left-hand gauntlet, still
Clasped empty in the other; and
One sees, with a sharp tender shock,
His hand withdrawn, holding her hand.

They would not think to lie so long.
Such faithfulness in effigy
Was just a detail friends would see:
A sculptor's sweet commissioned grace
Thrown off in helping to prolong
The Latin names around the base.

They would not guess how early in
Their supine stationary voyage
The air would change to soundless damage,
Turn the old tenantry away;
How soon succeeding eyes begin
To look, not read. Rigidly they

Persisted, linked, through lengths and breadths
Of time. Snow fell, undated. Light
Each summer thronged the glass. A bright
Litter of birdcalls strewed the same
Bone-riddled ground. And up the paths
The endless altered people came,
Washing at their identity.

Now, helpless in the hollow of
An unarmorial age, a trough
Of smoke in slow suspended skeins
Above their scrap of history,
Only an attitude remains:

Time has transfigured them into
Untruth. The stone fidelity
They hardly meant has come to be
Their final blazon, and to prove
Our almost-instinct almost true:
What will survive of us is love.

Philip Larkin

Noah

They gathered around and told him not to do it,
They formed a committee and tried to take control,
They cancelled his building permit and they stole
His plans. I sometimes wonder he got through it.
He told them wrath was coming, they would rue it,
He begged them to believe the tides would roll,
He offered them passage to his destined goal,
A new world. They were finished and he knew it.
All to no end.
                    And then the rain began.
A spatter at first that barely wet the soil,
Then showers, quick rivulets lacing the town,
Then deluge universal. The old man
Arthritic from his years of scorn and toil
Leaned from the admiral's walk and watched them drown.

Roy Daniells

Not Waving but Drowning

Nobody heard him, the dead man,
But still he lay moaning:
I was much further out than you thought
And not waving but drowning.

Poor chap, he always loved larking
And now he's dead.
It must have been too cold for him his heart gave way,
They said.

Oh, no no no, it was too cold always
(Still the dead one lay moaning)
I was much too far out all my life
And not waving but drowning.

Stevie Smith

The Lady of Shalott

PART I

On either side the river lie
Long fields of barley and of rye,
That clothe the wold and meet the sky;
And thro' the field the road runs by
    To many-tower'd Camelot;
And up and down the people go,
Gazing where the lilies blow
Round an island there below,
    The island of Shalott.

Willows whiten, aspens quiver,
Little breezes dusk and shiver
Thro' the wave that runs for ever
By the island in the river
    Flowing down to Camelot.
Four gray walls, and four gray towers,
Overlook a space of flowers,
And the silent isle imbowers
    The Lady of Shalott.

By the margin, willow-veil'd,
Slide the heavy barges trail'd
By slow horses; and unhail'd
The shallop flitteth silken-sail'd
    Skimming down to Camelot:
But who hath seen her wave her hand?
Or at the casement seen her stand?
Or is she known in all the land,
    The Lady of Shalott?

Only reapers, reaping early
In among the bearded barley,
Hear a song that echoes cheerly
From the river winding clearly,
    Down to tower'd Camelot:
And by the moon the reaper weary,
Piling sheaves in uplands airy,
Listening, whispers ''Tis the fairy
    Lady of Shalott.'

PART II

There she weaves by night and day
A magic web with colours gay.
She has heard a whisper say,
A curse is on her if she stay
     To look down to Camelot.
She knows not what the curse may be,
And so she weaveth steadily,
And little other care hath she,
     The Lady of Shalott.

Sometimes a troop of damsels glad,
An abbot on an ambling pad,
Sometimes a curly shepherd-lad,
Or long-hair'd page in crimson clad,
     Goes by to tower'd Camelot;
And sometimes thro' the mirror blue
The knights come riding two and two:
She hath no loyal knight and true,
     The Lady of Shalott.

But in her web she still delights
To weave the mirror's magic sights,
For often thro' the silent nights
A funeral, with plumes and lights,
    And music, went to Camelot:
Or when the moon was overhead,
Came two young lovers lately wed;
'I am half sick of shadows,' said
    The Lady of Shalott.

And moving thro' a mirror clear
That hangs before her all the year,
Shadows of the world appear.
There she sees the highway near
    Winding down to Camelot:
There the river eddy whirls,
And there the surly village-churls,
And the red cloaks of market girls,
    Pass onward from Shalott.

PART III

A bow-shot from her bower-eaves,
He rode between the barley-sheaves,
The sun came dazzling thro' the leaves,
And flamed upon the brazen greaves
    Of bold Sir Lancelot.
A red-cross knight for ever kneel'd
To a lady in his shield,
That sparkled on the yellow field,
    Beside remote Shalott.

The gemmy bridle glitter'd free,
Like to some branch of stars we see
Hung in the golden Galaxy.
The bridle bells rang merrily
    As he rode down to Camelot:
And from his blazon'd baldric slung
A mighty silver bugle hung,
And as he rode his armour rung,
    Beside remote Shalott.

All in the blue unclouded weather
Thick-jewell'd shone the saddle-leather,
The helmet and the helmet-feather
Burn'd like one burning flame together,
    As he rode down to Camelot,
As often thro' the purple night,
Below the starry clusters bright,
Some bearded meteor, trailing light,
    Moves over still Shalott.

His broad clear brow in sunlight glow'd;
On burnish'd hooves his war-horse trode;
From underneath his helmet flow'd
His coal-black curls as on he rode,
    As he rode down to Camelot.
From the bank and from the river
He flash'd into the crystal mirror,
'Tirra lirra,' by the river
    Sang Sir Lancelot.

She left the web, she left the loom,
She made three paces thro' the room,
She saw the water–lily bloom,
She saw the helmet and the plume,
    She look'd down to Camelot.
Out flew the web and floated wide;
The mirror crack'd from side to side;
'The curse is come upon me!' cried
    The Lady of Shalott.

PART IV

In the stormy east-wind straining,
The pale yellow woods were waning,
The broad stream in his banks complaining,
Heavily the low sky raining
     Over tower'd Camelot;
Down she came and found a boat
Beneath a willow left afloat,
And round about the prow she wrote
    The Lady of Shalott.

And down the river's dim expanse—
Like some bold seer in a trance,
Seeing all his own mischance—
With a glassy countenance
     Did she look to Camelot.
And at the closing of the day
She loosed the chain, and down she lay;
The broad stream bore her far away,
    The Lady of Shalott.

Lying, robed in snowy white
That loosely flew to left and right—
The leaves upon her falling light—
Thro' the noises of the night
     She floated down to Camelot:
And as the boat-head wound along
The willowy hills and fields among,
They heard her singing her last song,
    The Lady of Shallot.

Heard a carol, mournful, holy,
Chanted loudly, chanted lowly,
Till her blood was frozen slowly,
And her eyes were darken'd wholly,
     Turn'd to tower'd Camelot;
For ere she reach'd upon the tide
The first house by the water-side,
Singing in her song she died,
    The Lady of Shalott.

Under tower and balcony,
By garden-wall and gallery,
A gleaming shape she floated by,
Dead-pale between the houses high,
    Silent into Camelot.
Out upon the wharfs they came,
Knight and burgher, lord and dame,
And round the prow they read her name,
    The Lady of Shalott.

Who is this? and what is here?
And in the lighted palace near
Died the sound of royal cheer;
And they cross'd themselves for fear,
    All the knights at Camelot:
But Lancelot mused a little space;
He said, 'She has a lovely face;
God in His mercy lend her grace,
    The Lady of Shalott.'

Alfred, Lord Tennyson

The Lake Isle of Innisfree

I will arise and go now, and go to Innisfree,
And a small cabin build there, of clay and wattles made;
Nine bean rows will I have there, a hive for the honey bee,
And live alone in the bee-loud glade.

And I shall have some peace there, for peace comes dropping slow,
Dropping from the veils of the morning to where the cricket sings;
There midnight's all a glimmer, and noon a purple glow,
And evening full of the linnet's wings.

I will arise and go now, for always night and day
I hear lake water lapping with low sounds by the shore;
While I stand on the roadway, or on the pavements grey,
I hear it in the deep heart's core.

W. B. Yeats

Song

When I am dead, my dearest,
  Sing no sad songs for me;
Plant thou no roses at my head,
  Nor shady cypress tree:

Be the green grass above me
  With showers and dewdrops wet;
And if thou wilt, remember,
  And if thou wilt, forget.

I shall not see the shadows,
  I shall not feel the rain;
I shall not hear the nightingale
  Sing on, as if in pain;
And dreaming through the twilight
  That doth not rise nor set,
Haply I may remember,
  And haply may forget.

Christina Rossetti

Song

Stop all the clocks, cut off the telephone,
Prevent the dog from barking with a juicy bone,
Silence the pianos and with muffled drum
Bring out the coffin, let the mourners come.

Let aeroplanes circle moaning overhead
Scribbling on the sky the message He Is Dead,
Put crêpe bows round the white necks of the public doves,
Let the traffic policemen wear black cotton gloves.

He was my North, my South, my East and West,
My working week and my Sunday rest,
My noon, my midnight, my talk, my song;
I thought that love would last for ever: I was wrong.

The stars are not wanted now; put out every one,
Pack up the moon and dismantle the sun,
Pour away the ocean and sweep up the wood;
For nothing now can ever come to any good.

W. H. Auden

To the Virgins, to Make Much of Time

Gather ye rosebuds while ye may,
   Old Time is still a-flying:
And this same flower that smiles to-day
   To-morrow will be dying.

The glorious lamp of heaven, the sun,
   The higher he's a-getting,
The sooner will his race be run,
   And nearer he's to setting.

That age is best which is the first,
   When youth and blood are warmer;
But being spent, the worse, and worst
   Times still succeed the former.

Then be not coy, but use your time,
   And while ye may, go marry:
For having lost but once your prime,
   You may for ever tarry.

Robert Herrick

Leisure

What is this life if, full of care,
We have no time to stand and stare?

No time to stand beneath the boughs
And stare as long as sheep or cows.

No time to see, when woods we pass,
Where squirrels hide their nuts in grass.

No time to see, in broad daylight,
Streams full of stars, like skies at night.

No time to turn at Beauty's glance,
And watch her feet, how they can dance.

No time to wait till her mouth can
Enrich that smile her eyes began.

A poor life this if, full of care,
We have no time to stand and stare.

W. H. Davies

Naming of Parts

Today we have naming of parts. Yesterday,
We had daily cleaning. And tomorrow morning,
We shall have what to do after firing. But today,
Today we have naming of parts. Japonica
Glistens like coral in all of the neighbouring gardens,
   And today we have naming of parts.

This is the lower sling swivel. And this
Is the upper sling swivel, whose use you will see,
When you are given your slings. And this is the piling swivel,
Which in your case you have not got. The branches
Hold in the gardens their silent, eloquent gestures,
   Which in our case we have not got.

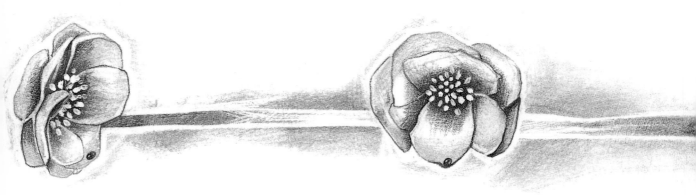

This is the safety-catch, which is always released
With an easy flick of the thumb. And please do not let me
See anyone using his finger. You can do it quite easy
If you have any strength in your thumb. The blossoms
Are fragile and motionless, never letting anyone see
   Any of them using their finger.

And this you can see is the bolt. The purpose of this
Is to open the breech, as you see. We can slide it
Rapidly backwards and forwards: we call this
Easing the spring. And rapidly backwards and forwards
The early bees are assaulting and fumbling the flowers:
    They call it easing the Spring.

They call it easing the Spring: it is perfectly easy
If you have any strength in your thumb: like the bolt,
And the breech, and the cocking-piece, and the point of balance,
Which in our case we have not got; and the almond-blossom
Silent in all of the gardens and the bees going backwards and for-
wards,
    For today we have naming of parts.

Henry Reed

Excelsior

The shades of night were falling fast,
As through an Alpine village passed
A youth, who bore, 'mid snow and ice,
A banner with the strange device,
   Excelsior!

His brow was sad; his eye beneath
Flashed like a faulchion from its sheath,
And like a silver clarion rung
The accents of that unknown tongue,
   Excelsior!

In happy homes he saw the light
Of household fire gleam warm and bright;
Above, the spectral glaciers shone,
And from his lips escaped a groan,
   Excelsior!

'Try not the Pass!' the old man said,
'Dark lowers the tempest overhead,
The roaring torrent is deep and wide!'
And loud that clarion voice replied,
   Excelsior!

'O stay!' the maiden said, 'and rest
Thy weary head upon this breast!'
A tear stood in his bright blue eye,
But still he answered, with a sigh,
   Excelsior!

'Beware the pine-tree's withered branch!
Beware the awful avalanche!'
This was the peasant's last goodnight!
A voice replied, far up the height,
   Excelsior!

At break of day, as heavenward
The pious monks of Saint Bernard
Uttered the oft-repeated prayer,
A voice cried through the startled air,
   Excelsior!

A traveller, by the faithful hound,
Half-buried in the snow, was found,
Still grasping in his hand of ice
That banner, with the strange device
   Excelsior!

There, in the twilight cold and grey,
Lifeless, but beautiful, he lay,
And from the sky, serene, and far,
A voice fell, like a falling star,
   Excelsior!

Henry Wadsworth Longfellow

Legend

The blacksmith's boy went out with a rifle
and a black dog running behind.
Cobwebs snatched at his feet,
rivers hindered him,
thorn branches caught at his eyes to make him blind
and the sky turned into an unlucky opal,
but he didn't mind,
I can break branches, I can swim rivers, I can stare out any spider I meet,
said he to his dog and his rifle.

The blacksmith's boy went over the paddocks
with his old black hat on his head.
Mountains jumped in his way,
rocks rolled down on him,
and the old crow cried, You'll soon be dead.
And the rain came down like mattocks.
But he only said
I can climb mountains, I can dodge rocks, I can shoot an old crow any day,
and he went on over the paddocks.

When he came to the end of the day the sun began falling.
Up came the night ready to swallow him,
like the barrel of the gun,
like an old black hat,
like a black dog hungry to follow him.
Then the pigeon, the magpie and the dove began wailing
and the grass lay down to billow him.
His rifle broke, his hat flew away and his dog was gone
and the sun was falling.

But in front of the night the rainbow stood on a mountain,
just as his heart foretold.
He ran like a hare,
he climbed like a fox;
he caught it in his hands, the colour and the cold—
like a bar of ice, like the column of a fountain,
like a ring of gold.
The pigeon, the magpie and the dove flew to stare,
and the grass stood up again on the mountain.

The blacksmith's boy hung the rainbow on his shoulder
instead of his broken gun.
Lizards ran out to see,
snakes made way for him,
and the rainbow shone as brightly as the sun.
All the world said, Nobody is braver, nobody is bolder,
nobody else has done
anything to equal it. He went home as bold as he could be
with the swinging rainbow on his shoulder.

Judith Wright

Jim Who Ran Away from his Nurse, and was Eaten by a Lion

There was a boy whose name was Jim;
His friends were very good to him.
They gave him tea, and cakes, and jam,
And slices of delicious ham,
And chocolate with pink inside,
And little tricycles to ride,
And read him stories through and through,
And even took him to the Zoo—
But there it was the dreadful fate
Befell him, which I now relate.

You know—at least you *ought* to know,
For I have often told you so—
That children never are allowed
To leave their nurses in a crowd;
Now this was Jim's especial foible,
He ran away when he was able,
And on this inauspicious day
He slipped his hand and ran away!
He hadn't gone a yard when—Bang!
With open jaws, a lion sprang,
And hungrily began to eat
The boy: beginning at his feet.

Now, just imagine how it feels
When first your toes and then your heels,
And then by gradual degrees,
Your shins and ankles, calves and knees,
Are slowly eaten, bit by bit.
No wonder Jim detested it!
No wonder that he shouted 'Hi!'
The honest keeper heard his cry,
Though very fat he almost ran
To help the little gentleman.
'Ponto!' he ordered as he came
(For Ponto was the lion's name),
'Ponto!' he cried, with angry frown
'Let go, Sir! Down, Sir! Put it down!'

The lion made a sudden stop,
He let the dainty morsel drop,
And slunk reluctant to his cage,
Snarling with disappointed rage.
But when he bent him over Jim,
The honest keeper's eyes were dim.
The lion having reached his head,
The miserable boy was dead!

When Nurse informed his parents, they
Were more concerned than I can say:—
His Mother, as she dried her eyes,
Said, 'Well—it gives me no surprise,
He would not do as he was told!'
His Father, who was self-controlled,
Bade all the children round attend
To James's miserable end,
And always keep a-hold of Nurse
For fear of finding something worse.

Hilaire Belloc

83

Adventures of Isabel

Isabel met an enormous bear,
Isabel, Isabel, didn't care;
The bear was hungry, the bear was ravenous,
The bear's big mouth was cruel and cavernous.
The bear said, Isabel, glad to meet you,
How do, Isabel, now I'll eat you!
Isabel, Isabel, didn't worry,
Isabel didn't scream or scurry.
She washed her hands and she straightened her hair up,
Then Isabel quietly ate the bear up.

Once in a night as black as pitch
Isabel met a wicked old witch.
The witch's face was cross and wrinkled,
The witch's gums with teeth were sprinkled.
Ho ho, Isabel! the old witch crowed,
I'll turn you into an ugly toad!
Isabel, Isabel, didn't worry,
Isabel didn't scream or scurry.
She showed no rage and she showed no rancor,
But she turned the witch into milk and drank her.

Isabel met a hideous giant,
Isabel continued self-reliant.
The giant was hairy, the giant was horrid,
He had one eye in the middle of his forehead.
Good morning, Isabel, the giant said,
I'll grind your bones to make my bread.
Isabel, Isabel, didn't worry,
Isabel didn't scream or scurry.
She nibbled the zwieback that she always fed off,
And when it was gone, she cut the giant's head off.

Isabel met a troublesome doctor,
He punched and he poked till he really shocked her.
The doctor's talk was of coughs and chills
And the doctor's satchel bulged with pills.
The doctor said unto Isabel,
Swallow this, it will make you well.
Isabel, Isabel, didn't worry,
Isabel didn't scream or scurry.
She took those pills from the pill concocter,
And Isabel calmly cured the doctor.

Ogden Nash

By St Thomas Water

By St Thomas Water
Where the river is thin
We looked for a jam-jar
To catch the quick fish in.
Through St Thomas Church-yard
Jessie and I ran
The day we took the jam-pot
Off the dead man.

On the scuffed tombstone
The grey flowers fell,
Cracked was the water,
Silent the shell.
The snake for an emblem
Swirled on the slab,
Across the beach of sky the sun
Crawled like a crab.

'If we walk,' said Jessie,
'Seven times round,
We shall hear a dead man
Speaking underground.'
Round the stone we danced, we sang,
Watched the sun drop,
Laid our heads and listened
At the tomb-top.

Soft as the thunder
At the storm's start
I heard a voice as clear as blood,
Strong as the heart.
But what words were spoken
I can never say,
I shut my fingers round my head,
Drove them away.

'What are those letters, Jessie,
Cut so sharp and trim
All round this holy stone
With earth up to the brim?'
Jessie traced the letters
Black as coffin-lead.
'He is not dead but sleeping,'
Slowly she said.

I looked at Jessie,
Jessie looked at me,
And our eyes in wonder
Grew wide as the sea.
Past the green and bending stones
We fled hand in hand,
Silent through the tongues of grass
To the river strand.

By the creaking cypress
We moved as soft as smoke
For fear all the people
Underneath awoke.
Over all the sleepers
We darted light as snow
In case they opened up their eyes,
Called us from below.

Many a day has faltered
Into many a year
Since the dead awoke and spoke
And we would not hear.
Waiting in the cold grass
Under a crinkled bough,
Quiet stone, cautious stone,
What do you tell me now?

Charles Causley

Do Not Go Gentle Into That Good Night

Do not go gentle into that good night,
Old age should burn and rave at close of day;
Rage, rage against the dying of the light.

Though wise men at their end know dark is right,
Because their words had forked no lightning they
Do not go gentle into that good night.

Good men, the last wave by, crying how bright
Their frail deeds might have danced in a green bay,
Rage, rage against the dying of the light.

Wild men who caught and sang the sun in flight,
And learn, too late, they grieved it on its way,
Do not go gentle into that good night.

Grave men, near death, who see with blinding sight
Blind eyes could blaze like meteors and be gay,
Rage, rage against the dying of the light.

And you, my father, there on the sad height,
Curse, bless, me now with your fierce tears, I pray.
Do not go gentle into that good night.
Rage, rage against the dying of the light.

Dylan Thomas

Follower

My father worked with a horse-plough,
His shoulders globed like a full sail strung
Between the shafts and the furrow.
The horses strained at his clicking tongue.

An expert. He would set the wing
And fit the bright steel-pointed sock.
The sod rolled over without breaking.
At the headrig, with a single pluck

Of reins, the sweating team turned round
And back into the land. His eye
Narrowed and angled at the ground,
Mapping the furrow exactly.

I stumbled in his hob-nailed wake,
Fell sometimes on the polished sod;
Sometimes he rode me on his back
Dipping and rising to his plod.

I wanted to grow up and plough,
To close one eye, stiffen my arm.
All I ever did was follow
In his broad shadow round the farm.

I was a nuisance, tripping, falling,
Yapping always. But today
It is my father who keeps stumbling
Behind me, and will not go away.

Seamus Heaney

Fern Hill

Now as I was young and easy under the apple boughs
About the lilting house and happy as the grass was green,
    The night above the dingle starry,
       Time let me hail and climb
    Golden in the heydays of his eyes,
And honoured among the wagons I was prince of the apple towns
And once below a time I lordly had the trees and leaves
       Trail with daisies and barley
    Down the rivers of the windfall light.

And as I was green and carefree, famous among the barns
About the happy yard and singing as the farm was home,
    In the sun that is young once only,
       Time let me play and be
    Golden in the mercy of his means,
And green and golden I was huntsman and herdsman, the calves
Sang to my horn, the foxes on the hills barked clear and cold,
       And the sabbath rang slowly
    In the pebbles of the holy streams.

All the sun long it was running, it was lovely, the hay
Fields high as the house, the tunes from the chimneys, it was air
    And playing, lovely and watery
        And fire green as grass.
    And nightly under the simple stars
As I rode to sleep the owls were bearing the farm away,
All the moon long I heard, blessed among stables, the nightjars
    Flying with the ricks, and the horses
        Flashing into the dark.

And then to awake, and the farm, like a wanderer white
With the dew, come back, the cock on his shoulder: it was all
    Shining, it was Adam and maiden,
        The sky gathered again
    And the sun grew round that very day.
So it must have been after the birth of the simple light
In the first, spinning place, the spellbound horses walking warm
    Out of the whinnying green stable
        On to the fields of praise.

And honoured among foxes and pheasants by the gay house
Under the new made clouds and happy as the heart was long,
    In the sun born over and over,
        I ran my heedless ways,
    My wishes raced through the house high hay
And nothing I cared, at my sky blue trades, that time allows
In all his tuneful turning so few and such morning songs
    Before the children green and golden
        Follow him out of grace.

Nothing I cared, in the lamb white days, that time would take me
Up to the swallow thronged loft by the shadow of my hand,
    In the moon that is always rising,
        Nor that riding to sleep
    I should hear him fly with the high fields
And wake to the farm forever fled from the childless land.
Oh as I was young and easy in the mercy of his means,
        Time held me green and dying
    Though I sang in my chains like the sea.

Dylan Thomas

The Woman of Water

There once was a woman of water
Refused a Wizard her hand.
So he took the tears of a statue
And the weight from a grain of sand
And he squeezed the sap from a comet
And the height from a cypress tree
And he drained the dark from midnight
And he charmed the brains from a bee
And he soured the mixture with thunder
And he stirred it with ice from hell
And the woman of water drank it down
And she changed into a well.

There once was a woman of water
Who was changed into a well
And the well smiled up at the Wizard
And down down down that old Wizard fell . . .

Adrian Mitchell

Tarantella

Do you remember an Inn,
Miranda?
Do you remember an Inn?
And the tedding and the spreading
Of the straw for a bedding,
And the fleas that tease in the High Pyrenees,
And the wine that tasted of the tar,
And the cheers and the jeers of the young muleteers
(Under the vine of the dark verandah)?
Do you remember an Inn, Miranda,
Do you remember an Inn?
And the cheers and the jeers of the young muleteers
Who hadn't got a penny,
And who weren't paying any,
And the hammer at the doors and the Din?

94

And the Hip! Hop! Hap!
Of the clap
Of the hands to the twirl and the swirl
Of the girl gone chancing,
Glancing,
Dancing,
Backing and advancing,
Snapping of the clapper to the spin
Out and in—
And the Ting, Tong, Tang of the Guitar!
Do you remember an Inn,
Miranda?
Do you remember an Inn?

Never more,
Miranda,
Never more.
Only the high peaks hoar:
And Aragon a torrent at the door.
No sound
In the walls of the Halls where falls
The tread
Of the feet of the dead to the ground,
No sound:
But the boom
Of the far Waterfall like Doom.

Hilaire Belloc

The Trees

The trees are coming into leaf
Like something almost being said;
The recent buds relax and spread,
Their greenness is a kind of grief.

Is it that they are born again
And we grow old? No, they die too.
Their yearly trick of looking new
Is written down in rings of grain.

Yet still the unresting castles thresh
In fullgrown thickness every May.
Last year is dead, they seem to say,
Begin afresh, afresh, afresh.

Philip Larkin

Loveliest of Trees

Loveliest of trees, the cherry now
Is hung with bloom along the bough,
And stands about the woodland ride
Wearing white for Eastertide.

Now, of my threescore years and ten,
Twenty will not come again,
And take from seventy springs a score,
It only leaves me fifty more.

And since to look at things in bloom
Fifty springs are little room,
About the woodlands I will go
To see the cherry hung with snow.

A. E. Housman

The Way Through the Woods

They shut the road through the woods
    Seventy years ago.
Weather and rain have undone it again,
    And now you would never know
There was once a road through the woods
    Before they planted the trees.

It is underneath the coppice and heath,
    And the thin anemones.
    Only the keeper sees
That, where the ring-dove broods,
    And the badgers roll at ease,
There was once a road through the woods.

Yet, if you enter the woods
    Of a summer evening late,
When the night-air cools on the trout-ringed pools
    Where the otter whistles his mate,
(They fear not men in the woods,
    Because they see so few)
You will hear the beat of a horse's feet
    And the swish of a skirt in the dew,
    Steadily cantering through
The misty solitudes,
    As though they perfectly knew
The old lost road through the woods. . . .
But there is no road through the woods.

Rudyard Kipling

Hawk Roosting

I sit in the top of the wood, my eyes closed.
Inaction, no falsifying dream
Between my hooked head and hooked feet:
Or in a sleep rehearse perfect kills and eat.

The convenience of the high trees!
The air's buoyancy and the sun's ray
Are of advantage to me;
And the earth's face upward for my inspection.

My feet are locked upon the rough bark.
It took the whole of Creation
To produce my foot, my each feather:
Now I hold Creation in my foot

Or fly up, and revolve it all slowly—
I kill where I please because it is all mine.
There is no sophistry in my body:
My manners are tearing off heads—

The allotment of death.
For the one path of my flight is direct
Through the bones of the living.
No arguments assert my right:

The sun is behind me.
Nothing has changed since I began.
My eye has permitted no change.
I am going to keep things like this.

Ted Hughes

Ozymandias

I met a traveller from an antique land
Who said: Two vast and trunkless legs of stone
Stand in the desert. . . . Near them, on the sand,
Half sunk, a shattered visage lies, whose frown,
And wrinkled lip, and sneer of cold command,
Tell that its sculptor well those passions read
Which yet survive, stamped on these lifeless things,
The hand that mocked them, and the heart that fed:
And on the pedestal these words appear:
'My name is Ozymandias, king of kings:
Look on my works, ye Mighty, and despair!'
Nothing beside remains. Round the decay
Of that colossal wreck, boundless and bare
The lone and level sands stretch far away.

Percy Bysshe Shelley

The Road not Taken

Two roads diverged in a yellow wood,
And sorry I could not travel both
And be one traveller, long I stood
And looked down one as far as I could
To where it bent in the undergrowth;

Then took the other, as just as fair,
And having perhaps the better claim,
Because it was grassy and wanted wear;
Though as for that the passing there
Had worn them really about the same,

And both that morning equally lay
In leaves no step had trodden black.
Oh, I kept the first for another day!
Yet knowing how way leads on to way,
I doubted if I should ever come back.

I shall be telling this with a sigh
Somewhere ages and ages hence:
Two roads diverged in a wood, and I—
I took the one less travelled by,
And that has made all the difference.

Robert Frost

The Terrrible Path

While playing at the woodland's edge
I saw a child one day,
She was standing near a foaming brook
And a sign half-rotted away.

There was something strange about her clothes;
They were from another age,
I might have seen them in a book
Upon a mildewed page.

She looked pale and frightened,
Her voice was thick with dread.
She spoke through lips rimmed with green
And this is what she said:

'I saw a signpost with no name,
I was surprised and had to stare,
It pointed to a broken gate
And a path that led nowhere.

'The path had run to seed and I
Walked as in a dream.
It entered a silent oak wood,
And crossed a silent stream.

'And in a tree a silent bird
Mouthed a silent song.
I wanted to turn back again
But something had gone wrong.

'The path would not let me go;
It had claimed me for its own,
It led me through a dark wood
Where all was overgrown.

'I followed it until the leaves
Had fallen from the trees,
I followed it until the frost
Drugged the autumn's bees.

'I followed it until the spring
Dissolved the winter snow,
And whichever way it turned
I was obliged to go.

'The years passed like shooting stars,
They melted and were gone.
But the path itself seemed endless,
It twisted and went on.

'I followed it and thought aloud,
"I'll be found, wait and see."
Yet in my heart I knew by then
The world had forgotten me.'

Frightened I turned homeward,
But stopped and had to stare.
I too saw that signpost with no name,
And the path that led nowhere.

Brian Patten

Uphill

Does the road wind uphill all the way?
   Yes, to the very end.
Will the day's journey take the whole long day?
   From morn to night, my friend.

But is there for the night a resting-place?
   A roof for when the slow, dark hours begin.
May not the darkness hide it from my face?
   You cannot miss that inn.

Shall I meet other wayfarers at night?
   Those who have gone before.
Then must I knock, or call when just in sight?
   They will not keep you standing at that door.

Shall I find comfort, travel-sore and weak?
   Of labour you shall find the sum.
Will there be beds for me and all who seek?
   Yea, beds for all who come.

Christina Rossetti

Stopping by Woods on a Snowy Evening

Whose woods these are I think I know.
His house is in the village though;
He will not see me stopping here
To watch his woods fill up with snow.

My little horse must think it queer
To stop without a farmhouse near
Between the woods and frozen lake
The darkest evening of the year.

He gives his harness bells a shake
To ask if there is some mistake.
The only other sound's the sweep
Of easy wind and downy flake.

The woods are lovely, dark and deep,
But I have promises to keep,
And miles to go before I sleep,
And miles to go before I sleep.

Robert Frost

You Are Old, Father William

'You are old, Father William,' the young man said,
  'And your hair has become very white;
And yet you incessantly stand on your head—
  Do you think, at your age, it is right?'

'In my youth,' Father William replied to his son,
  'I feared it might injure the brain;
But now that I'm perfectly sure I have none,
  Why, I do it again and again.'

'You are old,' said the youth, 'as I mentioned before,
  And have grown most uncommonly fat;
Yet you turned a back-somersault in at the door—
  Pray, what is the reason of that?'

'In my youth,' said the sage, as he shook his grey locks,
  'I kept all my limbs very supple
By the use of this ointment—one shilling the box—
  Allow me to sell you a couple.'

'You are old,' said the youth, 'and your jaws are too weak
    For anything tougher than suet;
Yet you finished the goose, with the bones and the beak—
    Pray, how did you manage to do it?'

'In my youth,' said his father, 'I took to the law,
    And argued each case with my wife;
And the muscular strength which it gave to my jaw
    Has lasted the rest of my life.'

'You are old,' said the youth; 'one would hardly suppose
    That your eye was as steady as ever;
Yet you balanced an eel on the end of your nose—
    What made you so awfully clever?'

'I have answered three questions, and that is enough,'
    Said his father; 'don't give yourself airs!
Do you think I can listen all day to such stuff?
    Be off, or I'll kick you down stairs!'

Lewis Carroll

I Am

I am—yet what I am, none cares or knows;
　My friends forsake me like a memory lost:
I am the self-consumer of my woes—
　They rise and vanish in oblivious host,
Like shadows in love's frenzied stifled throes
　And yet I am, and live—like vapours tost

Into the nothingness of scorn and noise,
　Into the living sea of waking dreams,
Where there is neither sense of life or joys,
　But the vast shipwreck of my life's esteems;
Even the dearest that I love the best
　Are strange—nay, rather, stranger than the rest.

I long for scenes where man hath never trod
　A place where woman never smiled or wept
There to abide with my Creator God,
　And sleep as I in childhood sweetly slept,
Untroubling and untroubled where I lie
　The grass below, above, the vaulted sky.

John Clare

On His Blindness

When I consider how my light is spent
Ere half my days, in this dark world and wide,
    And that one talent which is death to hide,
Lodged with me useless, though my soul more bent
To serve therewith my Maker, and present
    My true account, lest he, returning, chide;
    'Doth God exact day-labour, light denied?'
I fondly ask: but Patience, to prevent
    That murmur, soon replies, 'God doth not need
Either man's work, or his own gifts; who best
    Bear his mild yoke, they serve him best; his state
    Is kingly: thousands at his bidding speed,
And post o'er land and ocean without rest;
    They also serve who only stand and wait.'

John Milton

The Tiger

Tiger! Tiger! burning bright
In the forests of the night,
What immortal hand or eye
Could frame thy fearful symmetry?

In what distant deeps or skies
Burnt the fire of thine eyes?
On what wings dare he aspire?
What the hand dare seize the fire?

And what shoulder, and what art
Could twist the sinews of thy heart?
And, when thy heart began to beat,
What dread hand? and what dread feet?

What the hammer? what the chain?
In what furnace was thy brain?
What the anvil? what dread grasp
Dare its deadly terrors clasp?

When the stars threw down their spears,
And water'd heaven with their tears,
Did he smile his work to see?
Did he who made the lamb make thee?

Tiger! Tiger! burning bright
In the forests of the night,
What immortal hand or eye
Dare frame thy fearful symmetry?

William Blake

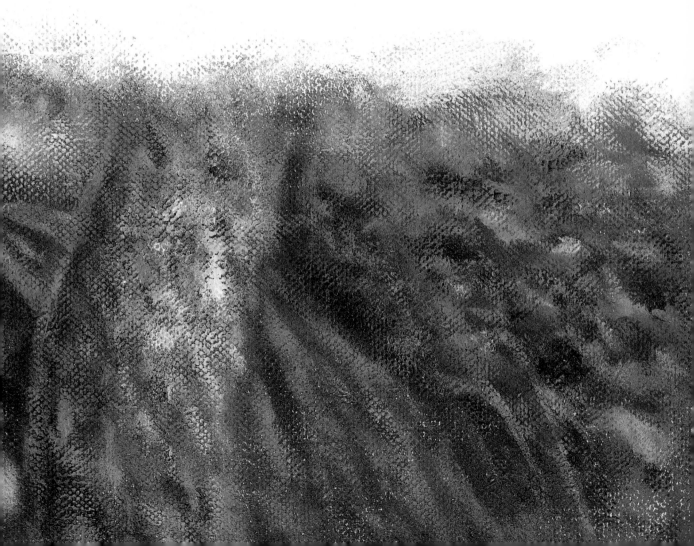

A Small Dragon

I've found a small dragon in the woodshed.
Think it must have come from deep inside a forest
because it's damp and green and leaves
are still reflecting in its eyes.

I fed it on many things, tried grass,
the roots of stars, hazel-nut and dandelion,
but it stared up at me as if to say, I need
foods you can't provide.

It made a nest among the coal,
not unlike a bird's but larger,
it is out of place here
and is quite silent.

If you believed in it I would come
hurrying to your house to let you share my wonder,
but I want instead to see
if you yourself will pass this way.

Brian Patten

Jabberwocky

'Twas brillig, and the slithy toves
Did gyre and gimble in the wabe;
All mimsy were the borogoves,
And the mome raths outgrabe.

Beware the Jabberwock, my son!
The jaws that bite, the claws that catch!
Beware the Jubjub bird and shun
The frumious Bandersnatch!

He took his vorpal sword in hand:
Long time the manxome foe he sought—
So rested he by the Tumtum tree,
And stood awhile in thought.

And as in uffish thought he stood,
The Jabberwock, with eyes of flame,
Came whiffling through the tulgey wood,
And burbled as it came!

One two! One two! and through and through
The vorpal blade went snicker-snack!
He left it dead, and with its head
He went galumphing back.

'And hast thou slain the Jabberwock!
Come to my arms, my beamish boy!
O frabjous day! Callooh! Callay!'
He chortled in his joy.

'Twas brillig, and the slithy toves
Did gyre and gimble in the wabe;
All mimsy were the borogoves,
And the mome raths outgrabe.

Lewis Carroll

Hunter Trials

It's awf'lly bad luck on Diana,
    Her ponies have swallowed their bits;
She fished down their throats with a spanner
    And frightened them all into fits.

So now she's attempting to borrow.
    Do lend her some bits, Mummy, *do*;
I'll lend her my own for to-morrow,
    But to-day *I'*ll be wanting them too.

Just look at Prunella on Guzzle,
    The wizardest pony on earth;
Why doesn't she slacken his muzzle
    And tighten the breech in his girth?

I say, Mummy, there's Mrs Geyser
    And doesn't she look pretty sick?
I bet it's because Mona Lisa
    Was hit on the hock with a brick.

Miss Blewitt says Monica threw it,
    But Monica says it was Joan,
And Joan's very thick with Miss Blewitt,
    So Monica's sulking alone.

And Margaret failed in her paces,
    Her withers got tied in a noose,
So her coronets caught in the traces
    And now all her fetlocks are loose.

Oh, it's me now. I'm terribly nervous.
   I wonder if Smudges will shy.
She's practically certain to swerve as
   Her Pelham is over one eye.

*   *   *

Oh wasn't it naughty of Smudges?
   Oh, Mummy, I'm sick with disgust
She threw me in front of the Judges,
   And my silly old collarbone's bust.

John Betjeman

Lochinvar

O young Lochinvar is come out of the west,
Through all the wide Border his steed was the best;
And save his good broadsword he weapons had none,
He rode all unarm'd, and he rode all alone.
So faithful in love, and so dauntless in war,
There never was knight like the young Lochinvar.

He staid not for brake, and he stopp'd not for stone,
He swam the Eske river where ford there was none;
But ere he alighted at Netherby gate,
The bride had consented, the gallant came late:
For a laggard in love, and a dastard in war,
Was to wed the fair Ellen of brave Lochinvar.

So boldly he enter'd the Netherby Hall,
Among bride's-men, and kinsmen, and brothers, and all:
Then spoke the bride's father, his hand on his sword,
(For the poor craven bridegroom said never a word,)
'O come ye in peace here, or come ye in war,
Or to dance at our bridal, young Lord Lochinvar?'

'I long woo'd your daughter, my suit you denied;—
Love swells like the Solway, but ebbs like its tide—
And now am I come, with this lost love of mine
To lead but one measure, drink one cup of wine.
There are maidens in Scotland more lovely by far,
That would gladly be bride to the young Lochinvar.'

The bride kiss'd the goblet: the knight took it up,
He quaff'd off the wine, and he threw down the cup.
She look'd down to blush, and she look'd up to sigh,
With a smile on her lips, and a tear in her eye.
He took her soft hand, ere her mother could bar,—
'Now tread we a measure!' said young Lochinvar.

So stately his form, and so lovely her face,
That never a hall such a galliard did grace;
While her mother did fret, and her father did fume,
And the bridegroom stood dangling his bonnet and plume;
And the bride-maidens whisper'd, ''Twere better by far
To have match'd our fair cousin with young Lochinvar.'

One touch to her hand, and one word in her ear,
When they reach'd the hall-door, and the charger stood near;
So light to the croupe the fair lady he swung,
So light to the saddle before her he sprung!
'She is won! we are gone, over bank, bush, and scaur;
They'll have fleet steeds that follow,' quoth young Lochinvar.

There was mounting 'mong Graemes of the Netherby clan;
Forsters, Fenwicks, and Musgraves, they rode and they ran:
There was racing and chasing on Cannobie Lee,
But the lost bride of Netherby ne'er did they see.
So daring in love, and so dauntless in war,
Have ye e'er heard of gallant like young Lochnivar?

Sir Walter Scott

The Horn

'Oh, hear you a horn, mother, behind the hill?
My body's blood runs bitter and chill.
The seven long years have passed, mother, passed,
And here comes my rider at last, at last.
I hear his horse now, and soon I must go.
How dark is the night, mother, cold the winds blow.
How fierce the hurricane over the deep sea!
For a seven years' promise he comes to take me.'

'Stay at home, daughter, stay here and hide.
I will say you have gone, I will tell him you died.
I am lonely without you, your father is old;
Warm is our hearth, daughter, but the world is cold.'

'Oh mother, Oh mother, you must not talk so.
In faith I promised, and for faith I must go,
For if that old promise I should not keep,
For seven long years, mother, I would not sleep.
Seven years my blood would run bitter and chill
To hear that sad horn, mother, behind the hill.
My body once frozen by such a shame
Would never be warmed, mother, at your hearth's flame.
But round my true heart shall the arms of the storm
For ever be folded, protecting and warm.'

James Reeves

The Highwayman

PART I

The wind was a torrent of darkness among the gusty trees,
The moon was a ghostly galleon tossed upon cloudy seas.
The road was a ribbon of moonlight over the purple moor,
And the highwayman came riding—
      Riding—riding—
The highwayman came riding, up to the old inn-door.

He'd a French cocked-hat on his forehead, a bunch of lace at his chin,
A coat of the claret velvet, and breeches of brown doe-skin.
They fitted with never a wrinkle. His boots were up to the thigh.
And he rode with a jewelled twinkle,
        His pistol butts a-twinkle,
His rapier hilt a-twinkle, under the jewelled sky.

Over the cobbles he clattered and clashed in the dark inn-yard.
He tapped with his whip on the shutters, but all was locked and barred.
He whistled a tune to the window, and who should be waiting there
But the landlord's black-eyed daughter,
        Bess, the landlord's daughter,
Plaiting a dark red love-knot into her long black hair.

And dark in the dark old inn-yard a stable-wicket creaked
Where Tim the ostler listened. His face was white and peaked.
His eyes were hollows of madness, his hair like mouldy hay,
But he loved the landlord's daughter,
        The landlord's red-lipped daughter.
Dumb as a dog he listened, and he heard the robber say—

'One kiss, my bonny sweetheart, I'm after a prize to-night,
But I shall be back with the yellow gold before the morning light;
Yet, if they press me sharply, and harry me through the day,
Then look for me by moonlight,
        Watch for me by moonlight,
I'll come to thee by moonlight, though hell should bar the way.'

He rose upright in the stirrups. He scarce could reach her hand,
But she loosened her hair i' the casement. His face burnt like a brand
As the black cascade of perfume came tumbling over his breast;
And he kissed its waves in the moonlight,
        (Oh, sweet black waves in the moonlight!)
Then he tugged at his rein in the moonlight, and galloped away to the west.

PART II

He did not come in the dawning. He did not come at noon;
And out o' the tawny sunset, before the rise o' the moon,
When the road was a gipsy's ribbon, looping the purple moor,
A red-coat troop came marching—
       Marching—marching—
King George's men came marching, up to the old inn-door.

They said no word to the landlord. They drank his ale instead.
But they gagged his daughter, and bound her, to the foot of her narrow bed.
Two of them knelt at her casement, with muskets at their side!
There was death at every window;
       And hell at one dark window;
For Bess could see, through her casement, the road that *he* would ride.

They had tied her up to attention, with many a sniggering jest.
They had bound a musket beside her, with the muzzle beneath her breast!
'Now, keep good watch!' and they kissed her.
       She heard the dead man say—
Look for me by moonlight;
       Watch for me by moonlight;
I'll come to thee by moonlight, though hell should bar the way!

She twisted her hands behind her; but all the knots held good!
She writhed her hands till her fingers were wet with sweat or blood!
They stretched and strained in the darkness, and the hours crawled by like years,
Till, now, on the stroke of midnight,
       Cold, on the stroke of midnight,
The tip of one finger touched it! The trigger at least was hers!

The tip of one finger touched it. She strove no more for the rest.
Up, she stood up to attention, with the muzzle beneath her breast.
She would not risk their hearing; she would not strive again;
For the road lay bare in the moonlight;
        Blank and bare in the moonlight;
And the blood of her veins, in the moonlight, throbbed to her love's refrain.

Tlot-tlot; tlot-tlot! Had they heard it? The horse-hoofs ringing clear;
Tlot-tlot, tlot-tlot, in the distance! Were they deaf that they did not hear?
Down the ribbon of moonlight, over the brow of the hill,
The highwayman came riding,
        Riding, riding!
The red-coats looked to their priming! She stood up, straight and still.

Tlot-tlot, in the frosty silence! *Tlot-tlot,* in the echoing night!
Nearer he came and nearer. Her face was like a light.
Her eyes grew wide for a moment; she drew one last deep breath,
Then her finger moved in the moonlight,
        Her musket shattered the moonlight,
Shattered her breast in the moonlight and warned him—with her death.

He turned. He spurred to the west; he did not know who stood
Bowed, with her head o'er the musket, drenched with her own red blood!
Not till the dawn he heard it, and his face grew grey to hear
How Bess, the landlord's daughter,
        The landlord's black-eyed daughter,
Had watched for her love in the moonlight, and died in the darkness there.

Back, he spurred like a madman, shouting a curse to the sky,
With the white road smoking behind him and his rapier brandished high.
Blood-red were his spurs i' the golden noon; wine-red was his velvet coat;
When they shot him down on the highway,
        Down like a dog on the highway,
And he lay in his blood on the highway, with the bunch of lace at his throat.

And still of a winter's night, they say, when the wind is in the trees,
When the moon is a ghostly galleon tossed upon cloudy seas,
When the road is a ribbon of moonlight over the purple moor,
A highwayman comes riding—
        Riding—riding—
A highwayman comes riding, up to the old inn-door.

Over the cobbles he clatters and clangs in the dark inn-yard.
And he taps with his whip on the shutters, but all is locked and barred.
He whistles a tune to the window, and who should be waiting there
But the landlord's black-eyed daughter,
        Bess, the landlord's daughter,
Plaiting a dark red love-knot into her long black hair.

Alfred Noyes

The Destruction of Sennacherib

The Assyrian came down like the wolf on the fold,
And his cohorts were gleaming in purple and gold;
And the sheen of their spears was like stars on the sea,
When the blue wave rolls nightly on deep Galilee.

Like the leaves of the forest when Summer is green,
That host with their banners at sunset were seen:
Like the leaves of the forest when Autumn hath blown,
That host on the morrow lay wither'd and strown.

For the Angel of Death spread his wings on the blast,
And breathed in the face of the foe as he pass'd;
And the eyes of the sleepers wax'd deadly and chill,
And their hearts but once heaved, and for ever grew still!

And there lay the steed with his nostril all wide,
But through it there roll'd not the breath of his pride;
And the foam of his gasping lay white on the turf,
And cold as the spray of the rock-beating surf.

And there lay the rider distorted and pale,
With the dew on his brow, and the rust on his mail:
And the tents were all silent, the banner alone,
The lances unlifted, the trumpet unblown.

And the widows of Ashur are loud in their wail,
And the idols are broke in the temple of Baal;
And the might of the Gentile, unsmote by the sword,
Hath melted like snow in the glance of the Lord!

Lord Byron

Abbey Tomb

I told them not to ring the bells
The night the Vikings came
Out of the sea and passed us by.
The fog was thick as cream
And in the abbey we stood still
As if our breath might blare
Or pulses rattle if we once
Stopped staring at the door.

Through the walls and through the fog
We heard them passing by.
The deafer monks thanked God too soon
And later only I
Could catch the sound of prowling men
Still present in the hills
So everybody else agreed
To ring the abbey bells.

And even while the final clang
Still snored upon the air,
And while the ringers joked their way
Down round the spiral stair,
Before the spit of fervent prayer
Had dried into the stone
The raiders came back through the fog
And killed us one by one.

Father Abbot at the altar
Lay back with his knees
Doubled under him, caught napping
In the act of praise.
Brother John lay unresponsive
In the warming room.
The spiders came out for the heat
And then the rats for him.

Under the level of the sheep
Who graze here all the time
We lie now, under tourists' feet
Who in good weather come.
I told them not to ring the bells
But centuries of rain
And blustering have made their tombs
Look just as right as mine.

Patricia Beer

129

Innocent's Song

Who's that knocking on the window,
Who's that standing at the door,
What are all those presents
Lying on the kitchen floor?

Who is the smiling stranger
With hair as white as gin,
What is he doing with the children
And who could have let him in?

Why has he rubies on his fingers,
A cold, cold crown on his head,
Why, when he caws his carol,
Does the salty snow run red?

Why does he ferry my fireside
As a spider on a thread,
His fingers made of fuses
And his tongue of gingerbread?

Why does the world before him
Melt in a million suns,
Why do his yellow, yearning eyes
Burn like saffron buns?

Watch where he comes walking
Out of the Christmas flame,
Dancing, double-talking:

Herod is his name.

Charles Causley

Say This City Has Ten Million Souls

Say this city has ten million souls,
Some are living in mansions, some are living in holes:
Yet there's no place for us, my dear, yet there's no place for us.

Once we had a country and we thought it fair,
Look in the atlas and you'll find it there:
We cannot go there now, my dear, we cannot go there now.

In the village churchyard there grows an old yew,
Every spring it blossoms anew:
Old passports can't do that, my dear, old passports can't do that.

The consul banged the table and said;
'If you've got no passport you're officially dead':
But we are still alive, my dear, but we are still alive.

Went to a committee; they offered me a chair;
Asked me politely to return next year:
But where shall we go to-day, my dear, but where shall we go to-day?

Came to a public meeting; the speaker got up and said:
'If we let them in, they will steal our daily bread';
He was talking of you and me, my dear, he was talking of you and me.

Thought I heard the thunder rumbling in the sky;
It was Hitler over Europe, saying: 'They must die';
O we were in his mind, my dear, O we were in his mind.

Saw a poodle in a jacket fastened with a pin,
Saw a door opened and a cat let in:
But they weren't German Jews, my dear, but they weren't German Jews.

Went down the harbour and stood upon the quay,
Saw the fish swimming as if they were free:
Only ten feet away, my dear, only ten feet away.

Walked through a wood, saw the birds in the trees;
They had no politicians and sang at their ease:
They weren't the human race, my dear, they weren't the human race.

Dreamed I saw a building with a thousand floors,
A thousand windows and a thousand doors;
Not one of them was ours, my dear, not one of them was ours.

Stood on a great plain in the falling snow;
Ten thousand soldiers marched to and fro:
Looking for you and me, my dear, looking for you and me.

W. H. Auden

In Time Of 'The Breaking Of Nations'

Only a man harrowing clods
   In a slow silent walk
With an old horse that stumbles and nods
   Half asleep as they stalk.

Only thin smoke without flame
   From the heaps of couch-grass;
Yet this will go onward the same
   Though Dynasties pass.

Yonder a maid and her wight
   Come whispering by:
War's annals will cloud into night
   Ere their story die.

Thomas Hardy

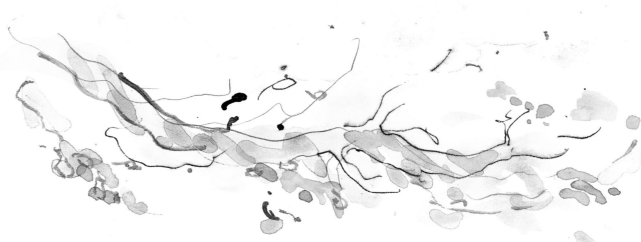

There Will Come Soft Rains

There will come soft rains and the smell of the ground,
And swallows calling with their shimmering sound;

And frogs in the pools singing at night,
And wild-plum trees in tremulous white;

Robins will wear their feathery fire
Whistling their whims on a low fence-wire;

And not one will know of the war, not one
Will care at last when it is done.

Not one would mind, neither bird nor tree,
If mankind perished utterly;

And Spring herself, when she woke at dawn,
Would scarcely know that we were gone.

Sara Teasdale

April Rain Song

Let the rain kiss you.
Let the rain beat upon your head with silver liquid drops.
Let the rain sing you a lullaby.

The rain makes still pools on the sidewalk.
The rain makes running pools in the gutter.
The rain plays a little sleep-song on our roof at night—

And I love the rain.

Langston Hughes

maggie and milly and molly and may

maggie and milly and molly and may
went down to the beach(to play one day)

and maggie discovered a shell that sang
so sweetly she couldn't remember her troubles, and

milly befriended a stranded star
whose rays five languid fingers were;

and molly was chased by a horrible thing
which raced sideways while blowing bubbles; and

may came home with a smooth round stone
as small as a world and as large as alone.

For whatever we lose(like a you or a me)
it's always ourselves we find in the sea

E. E. Cummings

Sea-Fever

I must down to the seas again, to the lonely sea and the sky,
And all I ask is a tall ship and a star to steer her by,
And a wheel's kick and the wind's song and the white sail's shaking,
And a grey mist on the sea's face and a grey dawn breaking.

I must down to the seas again, for the call of the running tide
Is a wild call and a clear call that may not be denied;
And all I ask is a windy day with the white clouds flying,
And the flung spray and the blown spume, and the seagulls crying.

I must down to the seas again, to the vagrant gypsy life,
To the gull's way and the whale's way where the wind's like a whetted knife;
And all I ask is a merry yarn from a laughing fellow-rover,
And quiet sleep and a sweet dream when the long trick's over.

John Masefield

On This Island

Look, stranger, on this island now
The leaping light for your delight discovers,
Stand stable here
And silent be,
And through the channels of the ear
May wander like a river
The swaying sound of the sea.

Here at a small field's ending pause
When the chalk wall falls to the foam and its tall ledges
Oppose the pluck
And knock of the tide,
And the shingle scrambles after the sucking surf,
And a gull lodges
A moment on its sheer side.

Far off like floating seeds the ships
Diverge on urgent voluntary errands,
And this full view
Indeed may enter
And move in memory as now these clouds do,
That pass the harbour mirror
And all the summer through the water saunter.

W. H. Auden

Cargoes

Quinquereme of Nineveh from distant Ophir
Rowing home to haven in sunny Palestine,
With a cargo of ivory,
And apes and peacocks,
Sandalwood, cedarwood, and sweet white wine.

Stately Spanish galleon coming from the Isthmus,
Dipping through the Tropics by the palm-green shores,
With a cargo of diamonds,
Emeralds, amethysts,
Topazes, and cinnamon, and gold moidores.

Dirty British coaster with a salt-caked smoke stack
Butting through the Channel in the mad March days,
With a cargo of Tyne coal,
Road-rail, pig-lead,
Firewood, iron-ware, and cheap tin trays.

John Masefield

A Smuggler's Song

If you wake at midnight, and hear a horse's feet,
Don't go drawing back the blind, or looking in the street,
Them that asks no questions isn't told a lie.
Watch the wall, my darling, while the Gentlemen go by!
    Five and twenty ponies
    Trotting through the dark—
    Brandy for the Parson,
    'Baccy for the Clerk;
    Laces for a lady, letters for a spy,
And watch the wall, my darling, while the Gentlemen go by!

Running round the woodlump if you chance to find
Little barrels, roped and tarred, all full of brandy-wine,
Don't you shout to come and look, nor use 'em for your play.
Put the brushwood back again—and they'll be gone next day!

If you see the stable-door setting open wide;
If you see a tired horse lying down inside;
If your mother mends a coat cut about and tore;
If the lining's wet and warm—don't you ask no more!

If you meet King George's men, dressed in blue and red,
You be careful what you say, and mindful what is said.
If they call you 'pretty maid', and chuck you 'neath the chin,
Don't you tell where no one is, nor yet where no one's been!

Knocks and footsteps round the house—whistles after dark—
You've no call for running out till the house-dogs bark.
Trusty's here, and *Pincher*'s here, and see how dumb they lie—
They don't fret to follow when the Gentlemen go by!

If you do as you've been told, 'likely there's a chance,
You'll be give a dainty doll, all the way from France,
With a cap of Valenciennes, and a velvet hood—
A present from the Gentlemen, along o' being good!
   Five and twenty ponies,
   Trotting through the dark—
   Brandy for the Parson,
   'Baccy for the Clerk.
Them that asks no questions isn't told a lie—
Watch the wall, my darling, while the Gentlemen go by!

Rudyard Kipling

The Forsaken Merman

Come, dear children, let us away;
Down and away below!
Now my brothers call from the bay,
Now the great winds shoreward blow,
Now the salt tides seaward flow;
Now the wild white horses play,
Champ and chafe and toss in the spray.
Children dear, let us away!
This way, this way!

Call her once before you go—
Call once yet!
In a voice that she will know:
'Margaret! Margaret!'
Children's voices should be dear
(Call once more) to a mother's ear;
Children's voices, wild with pain—
Surely she will come again!
Call her once and come away;
This way, this way!
'Mother dear, we cannot stay!
The wild white horses foam and fret.'
Margaret! Margaret!

Come, dear children, come away down;
Call no more!
One last look at the white-wall'd town,
And the little grey church on the windy shore;
Then come down!
She will not come though you call all day;
Come away, come away!

Children dear, was it yesterday
We heard the sweet bells over the bay?
In the caverns where we lay,
Through the surf and through the swell,
The far-off sound of a silver bell?
Sand-strewn caverns, cool and deep,
Where the winds are all asleep;
Where the spent lights quiver and gleam,
Where the salt weed sways in the stream,
Where the sea-beasts, ranged all round,
Feed in the ooze of their pasture-ground;
Where the sea-snakes coil and twine,
Dry their mail and bask in the brine;
Where great whales come sailing by,
Sail and sail, with unshut eye,
Round the world for ever and aye?
When did music come this way?
Children dear, was it yesterday?

Children dear, was it yesterday
(Call yet once) that she went away?
Once she sate with you and me,
On a red gold throne in the heart of the sea,
And the youngest sate on her knee.
She comb'd its bright hair, and she tended it well,
When down swung the sound of a far-off bell.
She sigh'd, she look'd up through the clear green sea;
She said: 'I must go, for my kinsfolk pray
In the little grey church on the shore to-day.
'Twill be Easter-time in the world—ah me!
And I lose my poor soul, Merman! here with thee.'
I said: 'Go up, dear heart, through the waves;
Say thy prayer, and come back to the kind sea-caves!'
She smiled, she went up through the surf in the bay.
Children dear, was it yesterday?

Children dear, were we long alone?
'The sea grows stormy, the little ones moan;
Long prayers,' I said, 'in the world they say;
Come!' I said; and we rose through the surf in the bay.
We went up the beach, by the sandy down
Where the sea-stocks bloom, to the white-wall'd town;
Through the narrow paved streets, where all was still,
To the little grey church on the windy hill.
From the church came a murmur of folk at their prayers,
But we stood without in the cold blowing airs.
We climb'd on the graves, on the stones worn with rains,
And we gazed up the aisle through the small leaded panes.
She sate by the pillar; we saw her clear:
'Margaret, hist! come quick, we are here!
Dear heart,' I said, 'we are long alone;
The sea grows stormy, the little ones moan.'
But, ah, she gave me never a look,
For her eyes were seal'd to the holy book!
Loud prays the priest; shut stands the door.
Come away, children, call no more!
Come away, come down, call no more!

Down, down, down!
Down to the depths of the sea!
She sits at her wheel in the humming town,
Singing most joyfully.
Hark what she sings: 'O joy, O joy,
For the humming street, and the child with its toy!
For the priest, and the bell, and the holy well;
For the wheel where I spun,
And the blessed light of the sun!'
And so she sings her fill,
Singing most joyfully,
Till the spindle drops from her hand,
And the whizzing wheel stands still.
She steals to the window, and looks at the sand,
And over the sand at the sea;
And her eyes are set in a stare;
And anon there breaks a sigh,
And anon there drops a tear,
From a sorrow-clouded eye,
And a heart sorrow-laden,
A long, long sigh;
For the cold strange eyes of a little Mermaiden
And the gleam of her golden hair.

Come away, away children;
Come children, come down!
The hoarse wind blows coldly;
Lights shine in the town.
She will start from her slumber
When gusts shake the door;
She will hear the winds howling,
Will hear the waves roar.
We shall see, while above us
The waves roar and whirl,
A ceiling of amber,
A pavement of pearl.
Singing: 'Here came a mortal,
But faithless was she!
And alone dwell for ever
The kings of the sea.'

But, children, at midnight,
When soft the winds blow,
When clear falls the moonlight,
When spring-tides are low;
When sweet airs come seaward
From heaths starr'd with broom,
And high rocks throw mildly
On the blanch'd sands a gloom;
Up the still, glistening beaches,
Up the creeks we will hie,
Over banks of bright seaweed
The ebb-tide leaves dry.
We will gaze, from the sand-hills,
At the white, sleeping town;
At the church on the hill-side—
And then come back down.
Singing: 'There dwells a loved one,
But cruel is she!
She left lonely for ever
The kings of the sea.'

Matthew Arnold

O Captain! My Captain!

O Captain! my Captain! our fearful trip is done,
The ship has weather'd every rack, the prize we sought is won,
The port is near, the bells I hear, the people all exulting,
While follow eyes the steady keel, the vessel grim and daring;
   But O heart! heart! heart!
     O the bleeding drops of red,
       Where on the deck my Captain lies,
         Fallen cold and dead.

O Captain! my Captain! rise up and hear the bells;
Rise up—for you the flag is flung—for you the bugle trills,
For you bouquets and ribbon'd wreaths—for you the shores a-crowding,
For you they call, the swaying mass, their eager faces turning;
   Here Captain! dear father!
     This arm beneath your head!
       It is some dream that on the deck,
         You've fallen cold and dead.

My Captain does not answer, his lips are pale and still,
My father does not feel my arm, he has no pulse nor will,
The ship is anchor'd safe and sound, its voyage closed and done,
From fearful trip the victor ship comes in with object won;
   Exult O shores, and ring O bells!
     But I with mournful tread,
       Walk the deck my Captain lies,
         Fallen cold and dead.

Walt Whitman

Casabianca

The boy stood on the burning deck,
    Whence all but he had fled;
The flame that lit the battle's wreck
    Shone round him o'er the dead.

Yet beautiful and bright he stood,
    As born to rule the storm;
A creature of heroic blood,
    A proud though childlike form.

The flames rolled on; he would not go
    Without his father's word;
That father, faint in death below,
    His voice no longer heard.

He called aloud, 'Say, Father, say,
    If yet my task be done!'
He knew not that the chieftain lay
    Unconscious of his son.

'Speak, Father!' once again he cried,
    'If I may yet be gone!'
And but the booming shots replied,
    And fast the flames rolled on.

Upon his brow he felt their breath,
    And in his waving hair,
And looked from that lone post of death
    In still yet brave despair;

And shouted but once more aloud,
    'My Father! must I stay?'
While o'er him fast, through sail and shroud,
    The wreathing fires made way.

They wrapped the ship in splendour wild,
   They caught the flag on high,
And streamed above the gallant child,
   Like banners in the sky.

There came a burst of thunder sound;
   The boy—Oh! where was he?
Ask of the winds, that far around
   With fragments strewed the sea—

With mast and helm and pennon fair,
   That well had borne their part—
But the noblest thing that perished there
   Was that young, faithful heart.

Felicia D. Hemans

La Belle Dame Sans Merci

'O what can ail thee, Knight-at-arms,
Alone and palely loitering?
The sedge is wither'd from the lake,
And no birds sing.

'O what can ail thee, Knight-at-arms,
So haggard and so woe-begone?
The squirrel's granary is full,
And the harvest's done.

'I see a lily on thy brow
With anguish moist and fever dew,
And on thy cheek a fading rose
Fast withereth too.'

'I met a lady in the meads
Full beautiful—a faery's child,
Her hair was long, her foot was light,
And her eyes were wild.

'I made a garland for her head,
And bracelets too, and fragrant zone;
She look'd at me as she did love,
And made sweet moan.

'I set her on my pacing steed,
And nothing else saw all day long,
For sidelong would she bend and sing
A faery's song.

'She found me roots of relish sweet,
And honey wild and manna dew,
And sure in language strange she said
"I love thee true."

She took me to her elfin grot,
And there she wept and sigh'd full sore;
And there I shut her wild wild eyes
With kisses four.

'And there she lulled me asleep,
And there I dream'd—Ah! woe betide!
The latest dream I ever dream'd
On the cold hill's side.

'I saw pale kings and princes too,
Pale warriors, death-pale were they all:
Who cried—"La belle Dame sans merci
Hath thee in thrall!"

'I saw their starv'd lips in the gloam
With horrid warning gaped wide,
And I awoke and found me here
On the cold hill's side.

'And this is why I sojourn here
Alone and palely loitering,
Though the sedge is wither'd from the lake,
And no birds sing.'

John Keats

The Listeners

'Is there anybody there?' said the Traveller,
  Knocking on the moonlit door;
And his horse in the silence champed the grasses
  Of the forest's ferny floor:
And a bird flew up out of the turret,
  Above the Traveller's head:
And he smote upon the door again a second time;
  'Is there anybody there?' he said.
But no one descended to the Traveller;
  No head from the leaf-fringed sill
Leaned over and looked into his grey eyes,
  Where he stood perplexed and still.
But only a host of phantom listeners
  That dwelt in the lone house then
Stood listening in the quiet of the moonlight
  To that voice from the world of men:
Stood thronging the faint moonbeams on the dark stair,
  That goes down to the empty hall,
Hearkening in an air stirred and shaken
  By the lonely Traveller's call.
And he felt in his heart their strangeness,
  Their stillness answering his cry,
While his horse moved, cropping the dark turf,
  'Neath the starred and leafy sky;
For he suddenly smote on the door, even
  Louder, and lifted his head:—
'Tell them I came, and no one answered,
  That I kept my word,' he said.

Never the least stir made the listeners,
  Though every word he spake
Fell echoing through the shadowiness of the still house
  From the one man left awake:
Ay, they heard his foot upon the stirrup,
  And the sound of iron on stone,
And how the silence surged softly backward,
  When the plunging hoofs were gone.

Walter de la Mare

The Hansel and Gretel House

When you come across it
you'll know better than to
nibble.
Who's there? asks the witch.
The wind, cry the
startled children.

A house may look sweet
from outside: beware!
Things happen in pretty houses
you wouldn't believe . . .

When the wind cries,
when the dog weeps,
when the voice of lost children
is heard in the wood,
let the forester hasten forth.

Gerda Mayer

To Any Reader

As from the house your mother sees
You playing round the garden trees,
So you may see, if you will look
Through the windows of this book,
Another child, far, far away,
And in another garden, play.
But do not think you can at all,
By knocking on the window, call
That child to hear you. He intent
Is all on his play-business bent.
He does not hear; he will not look,
Nor yet be lured out of his book.
For, long ago, the truth to say,
He has grown up and gone away,
And it is but a child of air
That lingers in the garden there.

Robert Louis Stevenson

Index of Titles and First Lines

First lines are in italics

Index of Authors

Index of Artists

Illustrations are by:

Sharon Bird pp 8, 36/37, 78/79, 100, 102/103, 116/117, 118, 127, 139, 150/151;

Hamish Blakely pp 25, 56/57, 71, 99, 110/111, 140/141;

Elaine Cox pp 16/17, 46/47, 52/53, 58/59, 74/75, 108/109, 136/137;

Lydia Evans pp 10/11, 54/55, 80/81, 94/95, 112/113, 128/129, 152/153;

Mary McQuillan pp 13, 14/15, 82/83, 84/85, 106/107, 114/115;

Charlie Mackesy pp 20/21, 30/31, 40/41, 89, 96/97, 105, 134/135, 154/155;

Alan Marks pp 18/19, 28/29, 32/33, 45, 48/49, 50/51, 72/73, 90/91, 92, 142/143, 144/145, 146;

Laurence Richardson pp 22/23, 26, 42/43, 76/77;

Sara van Niekerk pp 35, 39, 60/61, 86/87, 130/131, 133, 149.

The editors and publisher are grateful to Mrs Renate Keeping for kind permission to reproduce illustrations by the late Charles Keeping (on pp 63, 64/65, 66/67, 68, 120, 122, 125).

The cover illustration is by Elaine Cox (background) and Peter Melnyczuk (main picture).

Acknowledgements

The editors and publisher are grateful for permission to include the following copyright material:

John Agard: 'Prayer to Laughter' reprinted from *Laughter is an Egg* (Viking 1990), by kind permission of John Agard, c/o Caroline Sheldon Literary Agency. **W. H. Auden:** 'Night Mail', 'Twelve Songs IX' (Stop all the clocks . . .), 'Twelve Songs I' (Say This City . . .), and 'On This Island' reprinted from *Collected Poems* edited by Edward Mendelson, Copyright © 1976 by Edward Mendelson, William Meredith, and Monroe K. Spears, Executors of the Estate of W. H. Auden, by permission of Faber & Faber Ltd. and Random House Inc. **George Barker:** 'January Jumps About' reprinted from *To Aylsham Fair*, Copyright © George Barker 1970 (Faber), permission of Faber & Faber Ltd. **Patricia Beer:** 'Abbey Tomb' reprinted from *Collected Poems* (1988) by permission of Carcanet Press. **Hilaire Belloc:** 'Jim Who Ran Away from his Nurse and was Eaten by a Lion' and 'Tarantella', reprinted from *Complete Verse* (Pimlico), by permission of the Peters Fraser & Dunlop Group Ltd. **John Betjeman:** 'Hunter Trials' reprinted from *Collected Poems*, by permission of John Murray (Publishers) Ltd. **Roy Campbell:** 'Horses on the Camargue' reprinted from *Adamastor*. **Charles Causley:** 'By St Thomas Water' and 'Innocent's Song' reprinted from *Collected Poems* (Macmillan), by permission of David Higham Associates. **G. K. Chesterton:** 'The Donkey' reprinted from *Collected Poems* by permission of A. P. Watt Ltd on behalf of The Royal Literary Fund. **E. E. Cummings:** 'maggie and milly and molly and may' is reprinted from *Complete Poems 1904–1962*, edited by George J. Firmage, Copyright © 1956, 1984, 1991 by the Trustees for the E. E. Cummings Trust, by permission of W. W. Norton & Company Ltd. **Roy Daniells:** 'Noah' reprinted from *The Chequered Shade* (McLelland & Stewart), by permission of Laurenda Daniells. **W. H. Davies:** 'Leisure' reprinted from *The Collected Poems of W. H. Davies* (Cape), by permission of Random House UK Ltd. **Walter de la Mare:** 'Listeners' and 'Tartary' reprinted from *The Complete Poems of Walter de la Mare (1969)*, by permission of the Literary Trustees of Walter de la Mare and the Society of Authors as their representative. **U. A. Fanthorpe:** 'BC:AD', © U. A. Fanthorpe, reprinted from *Standing To* (Peterloo Poets 1982), by permission of Peterloo Poets. **Robert Frost:** 'The Road Not Taken' and 'Stopping by Woods on a Snowy Evening' reprinted from *The Poetry of Robert Frost* edited by Edward Connery Lathem, Copyright 1951 by Robert Frost, Copyright 1923 © 1969 by Henry Holt & Co., Inc., by permission of the publishers, Jonathan Cape/Random House UK Ltd. and Henry Holt and Co., Inc. **Thomas Hardy:** 'In Time of "The Breaking of Nations"' reprinted from *The Collected Poems of Thomas Hardy* (Macmillan). **Seamus Heaney:** 'Follower' reprinted from *Death of a Naturalist*, by permission of Faber & Faber Ltd., and from *Poems 1965–1975*, Copyright © 1980 by Seamus Heaney, by permission of Farrar, Straus & Giroux, Inc. **Russell Hoban:** 'Summer Recorded' reprinted from *The Pedalling Man* (Heinemann), by permission of David Higham Associates. **A. E. Housman:** 'Loveliest of Trees' reprinted from *A Shropshire Lad* (1896), by permission of The Society of Authors as the Literary representative of the Estate of A. E. Housman. **Langston Hughes:** 'April Rain Song' reprinted from *The Dream Keeper and Other Poems* (Alfred Knopf), Copyright 1932 by Alfred A. Knopf Inc. and renewed 1960 by Langston Hughes, by permission of the publisher,

Alfred A. Knopf, Inc., and David Higham Associates. **Ted Hughes:** 'Hawk Roosting' reprinted from *Lupercal*, by permission of Faber & Faber Ltd. **Rudyard Kipling:** 'The Way Through the Woods' from *Rewards and Fairies* and 'A Smuggler's Song' from *Puck of Pooks Hill* reprinted by permission of A. P. Watt Ltd on behalf of The National Trust for Places of Historic Interest or Natural Beauty. **Philip Larkin:** 'The Arundel Tomb' reprinted from *The Whitsun Weddings* and 'The Trees' from *High Windows*, by permission of Faber & Faber Ltd., and reprinted from *Collected Poems*, Copyright © 1988, 1989 by the Estate of Philip Larkin, by permission of Farrar, Straus & Giroux, Inc. **D. H. Lawrence:** 'Snake' reprinted from *The Complete Poems of D. H. Lawrence* edited by V. de Sola Pinto & F. W. Roberts, Copyright © 1964, 1971 by Angelo Ravagli and C. M. Weekley, Executors of the Estate of Frieda Lawrence Ravagli, by permission of Laurence Pollinger Ltd. and Viking Penguin, a division of Penguin Books USA Inc. for the Estate of Frieda Lawrence Ravagli. **Vachel Lindsay:** 'The Flower-fed Buffaloes' reprinted from *Going to the Stars*, (a Hawthorn Book), Copyright 1926 by D. Appleton & Co., renewed 1954 by Elizabeth C. Lindsay, by permission of Dutton Children's Books, a division of Penguin Books USA Inc., and from *Collected Poems* (Macmillan). **Roger McGough:** 'Waving at Trains' reprinted from *Waving at Trains* (Cape), by permission of the Peters Fraser & Dunlop Group Ltd. **John Masefield:** 'Sea Fever' and 'Cargoes' reprinted from *Poems* by permission of The Society of Authors as the literary representative of the Estate of John Masefield. **Gerda Mayer:** 'Hansel and Gretel House' first published in *Samphire* (1980), reprinted by permission of Gerda Mayer. **Adrian Mitchell:** 'The Woman of Water' reprinted from *Nothingmas Day* (Allison & Busby Ltd. 1984), by permission of the Peters Fraser & Dunlop Group Ltd. **Ogden Nash:** 'The Adventures of Isabel' reprinted from *Custard and Company*, Copyright © 1936 by Ogden Nash, Copyright © renewed, by permission of Curtis Brown Ltd., and Little, Brown and Company. **Alfred Noyes:** 'The Highwayman' reprinted from *Collected Poems*, by permission of John Murray (Publishers) Ltd. **Brian Patten:** 'The Terrible Path' reprinted from *Gargling with Jelly* by Brian Patten, Copyright © Brian Patten, 1985 (First published by Viking Children's Books 1985), by permission of Penguin Books Ltd. **Craig Raine:** 'A Martian Sends a Postcard Home', © Craig Raine 1979, reprinted from *A Martian Sends a Postcard Home* (OUP 1979), by permission of Oxford University Press. **Kathleen Raine:** 'Spell of Creation' reprinted from *The Year One* (1952) by permission of the author. **Henry Reed:** 'Naming of Parts' reprinted from *Collected Poems* edited by Jon Stallworthy (OUP 1991), by permission of Oxford University Press. **James Reeves:** 'The Horn', © James Reeves, reprinted from *Complete Poems for Children* (Heinemann), by permission of the Laura Cecil Literary Agency on behalf of the James Reeves Estate. **Stevie Smith:** 'Not Waving but Drowning' and 'The Galloping Cat' reprinted from *The Collected Poems of Stevie Smith* (Penguin Twentieth Century Classics), Copyright © 1972 by Stevie Smith, by permission of James MacGibbon and New Directions Publishing Corp. **Sara Teasdale:** 'There Will Come Soft Rains' reprinted from *Collected Poems* (Macmillan Publishing Co.). **Dylan Thomas:** 'Do Not Go Gentle Into That Good Night' and 'Fern Hill' reprinted from *The Poems* (J. M. Dent), by permission of David Higham Associates. **Judith Wright:** 'Legend' from *Collected Poems*, © Judith Wright 1971, 1994, reprinted by permission of HarperCollins Publishers Australia. **W. B. Yeats:** 'The Cat and the Moon', 'The Wild Swans at Coole', and 'The Lake Isle of Innisfree' reprinted from *Collected Poems* by permission of A. P. Watt Ltd on behalf of Michael Yeats.

Oxford University Press, Walton Street, Oxford OX2 6DP

Oxford   New York
Athens   Auckland   Bangkok   Bombay
Calcutta   Cape Town · Dar es Salaam   Delhi
Florence   Hong Kong   Istanbul   Karachi
Kuala Lumpur   Madras   Madrid   Melbourne
Mexico City   Nairobi   Paris   Singapore
Taipei   Tokyo   Toronto

and associated companies in
Berlin   Ibadan

Oxford is a trade mark of Oxford University Press

Library of Congress Catalog Card Number: 95-52205
A CIP catalogue record for this book is available from the British Library

ISBN 0 19 276120 X

Typesetting by Getset (BTS) Ltd, Eynsham, Oxford
Printed in Hong Kong